The Time Time Stopped

The Time Time Stopped

Don Gillmor

illustrations by
Ashley Spires

Scholastic Canada Ltd.
Toronto New York London Auckland Sydney
Mexico City New Delhi Hong Kong Buenos Aires

Scholastic Canada Ltd.
604 King Street West, Toronto, Ontario M5V 1E1, Canada

Scholastic Inc.
557 Broadway, New York, NY 10012, USA

Scholastic Australia Pty Limited
PO Box 579, Gosford, NSW 2250, Australia

Scholastic New Zealand Limited
Private Bag 94407, Botany, Manukau 2163, New Zealand

Scholastic Children's Books
Euston House, 24 Eversholt Street, London NW1 1DB, UK

Library and Archives Canada Cataloguing in Publication
Gillmor, Don
The time time stopped / Don Gillmor ; illustrations by
Ashley Spires.

ISBN 978-1-4431-0213-1

I. Spires, Ashley, 1978- II. Title.

PS8563.I59T55 2011   jC813'.54   C2011-902459-4

Cover image: © Shutterstock/Tom Mc Nemar and
(background) © Maliketh/istockphoto

Text copyright © 2011 by Don Gillmor
Illustrations copyright © 2011 by Ashley Spires

6 5 4 3 2 1   Printed in Canada 121   10 11 12 13 14

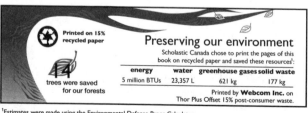

Printed on 15% recycled paper

Preserving our environment

Scholastic Canada chose to print the pages of this
book on recycled paper and saved these resources[1]:

energy	water	greenhouse gases	solid waste
5 million BTUs	23,357 L	621 kg	177 kg

Printed by **Webcom Inc.** on
Thor Plus Offset 15% post-consumer waste.

4 trees were saved
for our forests

FSC
www.fsc.org

MIX

Paper from
responsible sources

FSC® C004071

[1]Estimates were made using the Environmental Defense Paper Calculator.

For Justine and Cormac

Tristan

You couldn't imagine a worse month. Well, maybe you could. But Tristan Burberry couldn't. First, his family had moved to another city, a move that Tristan was completely and absolutely against. And if that wasn't bad enough, Tristan's older sister, Bella, took the best bedroom in the new house.

"Why do I get the worst bedroom?" Tristan asked.

"It's not the worst," his mother said, "it's more like . . . almost the best."

But Bella had the best.

And worse than all this, worse by far, was that they moved after the school year had already started, so even the new kids were starting to fit in. Tristan wasn't a new kid. He was a *new* new kid.

And worse — the final worse — he was the *only* new new kid.

So he sat in his room, unhappy about being in a new city, a new school, a new house and a new (worst) bedroom.

His mother, who had been looking for reasons that Tristan might like the new city, had told him that it had a zoo. Tristan liked animals, and the city where they used to live didn't have one, and she had promised him (again) they would go to this zoo on Saturday.

So on Saturday morning, the last normal Saturday he would experience for some time, Tristan woke up with high hopes. He got dressed and went downstairs for breakfast.

His mother was dressed for work and she was heading out the front door.

Tristan was shocked.

"What about the zoo?" he asked her.

"Oh, sweetheart," his mother said. "Maybe next week."

"That's what you said *last* week."

"The animals aren't going anywhere, dear."

"Neither are we," Tristan said.

"I'm sorry, sweetheart, it's been so busy at work. I just don't have the time." His mother checked her pockets for her keys and looked at herself in the hall mirror. She pushed a few hairs into place. "Must rush," she said, kissing the top of his head then closing the door behind her.

He heard her car tear out of the driveway.

His father suddenly came running out of the kitchen, balancing a briefcase, a cup of coffee, a piece of toast, the morning paper and a cellphone. He put the whole piece of toast into his mouth and tried to talk into the phone.

"Humpsturr murp mugle snumpwart."

"Dad, I . . ."

"No time, sport," his dad said, swallowing the toast. He ran out the door.

"But it's Saturday," Tristan yelled after him. "It's a *holiday*."

"Every day's a holiday when you're a kid," his father yelled back. "Your sister's going to take you to the mall. Won't that be great?" He ran for the bus stop like an Olympic sprinter.

Bella was twelve and was only nice to Tristan when there was someone around to see her being nice.

What's the point of being nice if there aren't any witnesses? She was in the kitchen, combing her hair and eating pizza for breakfast and reading a magazine.

"Do we have to go to the mall?" Tristan asked. "Wouldn't you rather go to the zoo?"

"Tristan, the zoo is full of *animals*."

"That's the whole point."

"I'm meeting my friends at the mall. Don't do anything to embarrass me. So, don't do *anything*."

They took the bus to the mall and Bella met her friends Sarah and Boink — whose real name wasn't Boink, but it was something almost as weird, which Tristan had forgotten. All three girls were dressed the same, and they went to forty-two stores and tried on clothes and all talked at once. His sister had made friends on the first day of school, another thing about her that bothered him. He hadn't made any friends.

Tristan walked ten steps behind his sister, as he had been instructed. ("If you get any closer, even *nine* steps, then I'm not going to buy you any lunch," she had warned him.) He stood outside forty-two stores and stared at the people going by. Six women asked him if he was lost.

At one store, Bella tried on fourteen sweaters in a row. "Is this too . . . I don't know," she said, turning sideways in the mirror. "Maybe the colour's wrong, or . . ."

Or *you* are wrong, Tristan thought to himself. Or the *mall* is wrong, or *everything* is wrong.

"It's too . . . too something," Bella said.

Too stupid, thought Tristan. That's the word you're looking for. It's too stupid.

Bella gave Tristan a look, like she could hear his thoughts. Which gave Tristan the creeps.

The girls tried on T-shirts, shoes and jeans. Blue jeans, white jeans, pink jeans, jeans that were ripped, jeans with stains, jeans with holes, jeans that were barely even jeans anymore.

They didn't go to the toy store, or the sporting goods store, or the pet store.

"Can we go to the sports store?" Tristan asked.

"No," Bella said. "We can't."

By noon, Tristan was getting hungry.

"Can we go and have lunch?" he asked his sister.

Bella gave him a look.

"I'm hungry," he said.

"Whatever," Bella said.

They went to the food court and spent an hour looking at the menus of the different restaurants. They finally bought Quickie Burgers and Tristan sat at a separate table while Bella and her friends whispered and giggled and pointed at everyone who walked by. After lunch they walked around for what seemed like three days. They looked at posters for movies that were playing at the megaplex then didn't go and see any of them. Tristan had an orange drink that he got from a hut shaped like an orange, though the drink didn't actually taste like oranges. He counted the number of people wearing red hats (thirty-nine), tried on an itchy brown sweater at a store that Boink took him to, and counted the number of people he thought might be aliens (thirty-nine). They finally sat at the fountain in the middle of the mall.

"Can we go now?" Tristan asked after a few minutes.

"We're not finished," Bella said.

"Not finished *what*?" Tristan asked. "We're not even *doing* anything. We're just killing time."

"Time's not dead until I say it is," Bella replied.

Tristan and Bella stayed until the mall closed. They were the last to leave; the stores were turning out their lights. Bella had bought a T-shirt, which she thought was cool three hours ago, but now she wasn't so sure.

"What do you want to do now?" Bella asked her friends.

"My mom's expecting me for dinner," Sarah said. "I'd invite you over, except . . ." She nodded in the direction of Tristan, who was standing ten steps to the side.

"I have to go too," Boink said.

"Come on, Tristan," Bella called over to him. "We're going home now."

Tristan was relieved. It had been the longest day of his life. He and Bella got on a bus and sat three seats apart.

At home Bella took a frozen dinner out for Tristan. Tristan read the box, which said, "NEW IMPROVED sugar-free packaging, organic-looking, chicken-flavoured, pizza-shaped . . ." He couldn't read the small print after that. Bella put it in the microwave for five minutes, then put it on the table and left to watch TV.

Tristan took a bite. "It's still cold in the middle," he said.

"That's why they're called frozen dinners, Einstein," his sister said.

Bella watched TV, clicking the channel changer every five seconds for two hours. "There's nothing on TV," she finally said, and went up to her bedroom.

Tristan stayed downstairs and played with his Merlin Super Magic Box. It was supposed to do all kinds of magical things. Except it didn't. It didn't do anything magical. Which was the problem with so many things in the world, he thought. They didn't do what you thought they would. They weren't magic. He finally fell asleep on the living room floor.

And that's where his parents found him when they came home an hour later.

"Oh, look," his mother said. "The poor dear." She picked him up and carried him up the stairs and put him in his bed.

Guilty

So that was Tristan Burberry's weekend. A lot of weekends were like that. He didn't know why they were called weekends. Maybe, he thought, they should come up with another name, like *week-endless,* because it felt like his whole life was one super big week that went on forever.

Monday arrived and to Tristan it looked a lot like Saturday and Sunday: his mother rushing out the door, his dad talking with his mouth full of toast. The only difference was that he was going to school, which couldn't be any worse than going to the mall with his sister.

On the school bus, Tristan had to sit beside Burt Lump, who was the school bully and looked like a huge potato with arms and legs. His head sat like a (slightly) smaller potato on top. Why was it, Tristan wondered, that every school had a bully? Why couldn't there be a special school that was only for bullies, and then the rest of them would be safe and the bullies could bully each other? How would that work? Tristan wondered. Would they take turns bullying each other?

Lump was also the guiltiest-looking guy in the school. The reason he looked guilty is that, most of the time, he *was*. He was big and mean and guilty, and everyone sat as far away from him as possible, and that's why the only seat left on the bus was beside him.

"I didn't do it," Lump said.

Which is what he always said, and it was usually a sign that he had done it, whatever *it* was.

"Didn't do what?" Tristan asked.

"If, like . . ." Lump said, "there were one or more garter snakes slithering around on the floor of this bus, I didn't let them out."

Tristan looked at him. Then he looked down to see two garter snakes slithering down the aisle of the bus. He waited for the screams.

He didn't have to wait long.

The screams got louder and became one big scream as everyone joined in.

The driver stopped the bus. He picked up the two garter snakes (which Tristan knew were actually pretty friendly) and threw them out onto the grass. Then he walked down the aisle and stood over Tristan and Lump.

"Lump."

"I didn't do it."

"No, of course not. It was probably one of the girls. That's my guess." The bus driver was named Mr. Dobbins and he had a red face that looked like it could explode at any minute.

"Maybe Tristan did it," Lump said. "He knows a lot about snakes."

"Did you put snakes on the bus, Tristan?" Dobbins asked.

"*No*," Tristan said quickly. "I *didn't*."

A snake slithered by. A girl screamed.

Dobbins picked up the snake and threw it out onto the grass with the other two and then drove to school.

Lump was the kind of boy who could get you into trouble just by being near him. And it was Tristan's bad luck to sit beside him. He seemed to have a lot of bad luck.

School

Tristan sat at his desk and searched for his math book. He couldn't find it, though he noticed everyone else in the class had found theirs.

Ms Barkley, who had a voice like a door slamming, said, "Now, class. Please direct your attention to the blackboard."

On the blackboard was a large chalk drawing of a teacher who looked sort of like Ms Barkley (her name was printed underneath so people could be sure it was her) and there was a speech bubble like you see in cartoons and inside the bubble were the words: I AM AN IDIOT.

Lump leaned over to Tristan and whispered, "I didn't do it. But I know who did."

Tristan looked at him.

"*You* did," Lump said, then smiled a very unfortunate smile.

"*Tristan Burberry!*" Ms Barkley said in her door-slamming voice.

"Yes, Ms Barkley."

"I've told you before not to talk to your neighbour."

"I wasn't talking, Ms Barkley."

"I just *saw* you talking, Tristan. Do you think I *imagined* it?"

What she had seen was him listening, but this didn't matter. Tristan knew from experience that there wasn't any point in arguing with your teacher. He was in trouble.

"Did you draw this, Tristan?"

"No, Ms Barkley."

"Hmm . . . . Well, it didn't draw itself. Perhaps you'd like to come up and erase it."

He didn't want to go up and erase it. For one thing, erasing it would make him look guilty, like he was the one who had drawn it. But the other reason was that he was the new kid and everyone would be staring at him and he'd be embarrassed, and when he got embarrassed his face got very hot and very red and that made him even more embarrassed, because he knew people were staring at his very red face. So he was even embarrassed by being embarrassed.

"But I didn't draw it, Ms Barkley. It's not fair."

"*Fair? Not fair?* Do you think that it was *fair* that I should start my day by walking into the classroom and seeing this horrible drawing on the blackboard? It doesn't even look like me."

"No, but . . ."

"Few things are fair, Tristan. *Life's* not fair. Now please come up and erase this ghastly drawing."

Tristan walked up to the front of the class and he could feel his face getting redder and hotter and he felt like those few minutes up there lasted an hour. He walked back to his desk and noticed that Lump was smiling his horrible smile. "Way to go, Fire-Engine-Face," he whispered.

"Shall we begin our class?" Ms Barkley said. "Who can tell me what six times eight is. Anyone?"

Tristan knew the answer (forty-eight) and put up his hand, hoping it would make him seem less like the kind of person who would put a rude drawing of the teacher on the blackboard. But Elaine Twofer also put up her hand. Ms Barkley made a point of looking around the class at the two hands that were up, but Tristan knew, and Elaine Twofer knew, and Ms Barkley knew, that she would pick Elaine. Which she did. "Elaine, can you tell us. Six times eight."

"Forty-eight, Ms Barkley."

"That's absolutely right, Elaine. Thank you *so* much."

At lunch, Tristan sat by himself. Bella was sitting on the other side of the lunchroom with all her new friends.

Burt Lump came lumbering in and sat down heavily beside Tristan like a giant sandbag that had fallen out of an airplane. His face looked both angry and scheming.

"Blueberry, I have an idea."

Any idea of Lump's meant someone would get in trouble. And that someone would probably be Tristan.

"We change all the clocks in the school," Lump said. "We do it at lunchtime. Instead of eating our lunch, we go to every room and change the clock so it says three-thirty, and then all the teachers will think the day is over and let us out. It's a brilliant plan."

"Don't you think they'll be wearing watches?" Tristan could see that Lump hadn't thought of that. His face looked, suddenly, like a dark cloud.

"We'll cross that bridge when we come to it," Lump said. "And you're going to help me, Blueberry." His face got even darker. "Because if you don't, you'll *get it.* Got it? Good." He got up and left Tristan sitting by himself. Tristan ate his lunch alone and it seemed like he was sitting there for two hours.

The afternoon dragged on. It moved slower than a hippopotamus walking underwater (which Tristan had seen on TV, and they are very slow). Each minute lasted an hour, each hour felt like a day. Tristan stared at the clock. At one point he thought the minute hand might have moved *backwards.*

"Tristan," Ms Barkley said. "Staring at the clock isn't going to make the time go faster."

"No, Ms Barkley."

It was warm in their classroom. The sun came in through the large windows and Tristan found himself getting so sleepy he couldn't keep his eyes open. He tried pinching himself to stay awake but even that wasn't enough. He nodded off and when he woke up he hoped that three hours had gone by and couldn't believe that less than a minute had disappeared.

When the class was finally over, Tristan was relieved. But his relief didn't last long when he realized that he didn't really have much else to do. He didn't have any friends to hang out with. And his parents didn't get home until much later. They spent even more time at their new jobs than they had spent at their old jobs, which was a lot. His mother said that it was because with any new thing it took a while to get used to it and that he would understand when he was older. She said they'd be settled in soon and then both she and his father would be coming home earlier.

Tristan walked home from the bus stop slowly. Up ahead, Bella was walking with her friends. He could see them whispering and laughing. He was careful not to go too fast because Bella had told him that if he ever went anywhere near her when she was with her friends then she would make the rest of his life miserable. And at this point, at least, it looked like she could do it.

At home, he turned on the TV to watch his favourite show, *Nature Hour with Lulu Adams*. Lulu Adams didn't seem much older than Bella but got to go all over the world to look at animals and then explain everything about them. For example, elephants can live to be seventy years old, and their trunks have thousands of muscles in them. Tristan wished Lulu was his sister instead of Bella. Then maybe he could go with her to Africa to watch how fast a cheetah ran (112 kilometres an hour) or go to the Arctic and see how big the polar bear was (680 kilograms).

"This week," Lulu Adams said, smiling on the TV screen, "we're going to look at the fascinating world of the king cobra, one of the largest and deadliest snakes in the world. Don't go away!"

"The king cobra!" Tristan shouted. It was one of his favourite snakes.

Just then Bella flopped onto the couch beside him. She grabbed the channel changer and turned to a show called *Zombie Days*, about four teenagers who all worked in a mall.

"Bella!" Tristan shrieked. "They're going to do the king cobra on *Nature Hour*. It's my *favourite!*"

"Tristan, I've got homework to do. You know I have to have the TV on to do my homework. You'll understand when you're older."

Why did people keep telling him he would understand when he was older? Was there some magic age when you suddenly understood everything, and if there was, then why was he wasting his time in Ms Barkley's class? And why was there so much Bella didn't understand? Like everything?

"I won't understand when I'm older!" he said. "Why can't you go somewhere else and do it?"

"Because I need the distraction."

This didn't make any sense to Tristan.

"Well, then, if it's just a distraction, why don't we watch *Nature Hour with Lulu Adams?*"

"I'm not watching a show about snakes, Tristan. It's too creepy."

"But you're not even *watching*. You just want a distraction!"

"But the *right* distraction."

They only had one television, which his parents said would be good because then they'd have to learn to share. Except his sister hadn't learned anything about sharing and it was obvious to Tristan that she never would.

"When are Mom and Dad getting home?" Tristan asked.

"They said to make dinner without them. There's something in the freezer."

"What is it?"

"I don't know. Something. I'll go look later. Leave me alone and let me finish my homework."

Tristan went up to his room and sort of half-played with his toys. He built part of a pirate ship, drew half of a drawing, then pulled out the Monopoly set and looked at it. He read part of a book about mammals and put tape on his hockey stick. He stared out the window and watched a leaf fall onto the grass.

He ate dinner.

He slept.

The Curious Lull

In the morning, Tristan watched his parents race around frantically getting ready for work. Most of the time he was asleep when they got home, and in the mornings they were too busy to talk to him. Tristan wondered if he was disappearing somehow. No one noticed him, and whenever he said anything, no one listened anyway. (And when they did listen, like Ms Barkley, they didn't believe him.)

"I had thirty-two chocolate bars for breakfast," he said to his mother.

"Where are those *keys* of mine?" she said, throwing things out of her purse. "Yes, breakfast, good good, important meal, Tristan."

"I'm going to buy a motorcycle and race it up and down the street today. Instead of going to school."

"I am so *so* late. School, yes, wonderful, Tristan."

His mother charged out the door. "Must rush, *must rush*. Kiss, kiss, children," she said over her shoulder.

His dad came bolting out of the kitchen balancing two phones, his toast and coffee. "Hey, sport!" he said.

"Bella married a circus clown yesterday," Tristan said.

"Hmm, what, good, circus." His dad was looking through his briefcase for some papers and spilling coffee onto his shoes.

"They're moving to New Zealand. So that's great news."

"Great news," his dad repeated, as he quickly flipped through his papers.

"I sent away for a pet killer whale."

Both his dad's phones were ringing. "Terrific, son. Killer diller."

"We need to build a pool. It'll cost two million dollars."

His dad barked into one of his phones, "I can't . . . There isn't . . . What kind of *birdbrain* . . . Stan, hang on a sec." His dad gathered all his things and ran out the door, yelling over his shoulder. "Glad you're having a whale of a time and getting killer grades, sport. I told you the new school . . ."

Then he was gone.

Bella was supposed to walk him to the school bus stop, but she made him stay ten steps behind her because she didn't want her new friends to see her walking with her little brother.

On the bus, Burt Lump said, "I have a new plan." Tristan knew there was no point in telling Lump he didn't want to hear his dumb plan, because Lump would tell him anyway.

"We change the clocks," Lump said. "We make them all say three-thirty. The teachers think something's wrong — it can't be *that* late! — and they look down at their watches to check the time, and . . . they're gone!"

Tristan looked at Lump's alarmingly guilty potato face.

"You know why their watches are gone?" Lump asked. "I'll tell you why, Blueberry. Because *you* stole them."

"*Me?*"

"Your job is to steal the watches while I'm changing the clocks."

"But I'm not a thief," Tristan said. "I don't want to steal the teachers' watches."

"It doesn't matter if you *want* to," Lump said, his

beady eyes boring into Tristan. "You're *going* to. If you don't . . ." and he paused for a moment, like he was trying to think up a suitable punishment in his small brain, ". . . then I'll *get* you." And then he added, with that horrible smile, "I got the last new kid. I got him good. Why do you think that seat was empty? Yeah. Think about *that*, Blueberry."

They sat in silence until they got to the school. The trip seemed to take an hour.

In Ms Barkley's class the minutes ticked by as she told the class about why numbers were so fascinating, and how they were your friends and you just had to get to know them and then you'd see that you really liked them. They were like people that way.

But Tristan couldn't think about making friends with numbers (though at this point he'd be happy to make friends with just about anything, even a number). All he could think about was Lump and his threats and those teachers' watches. If he didn't steal them, then Lump would beat him up or do something worse, and then he'd steal them himself and blame Tristan, and who would believe Tristan?

Who could he go to with this problem? Not his parents, who were never home and didn't hear what he said even when they were. Not Ms Barkley, who didn't believe him, even when he was telling the truth. And certainly not his sister, who he couldn't even walk with, let alone talk to. And he didn't have any friends to tell. The odd thing was, Burt Lump was the closest thing he had to a friend, and he couldn't go to Lump and complain about Lump. *Hey, Lump, there's this guy who's a bully and his name is Lump and he's ruining my life. What should I do about him?*

So Tristan thought about those watches. How would you go about stealing watches off teachers' wrists? Even the world's greatest magician couldn't do it. As he sat in class, he looked at Ms Barkley's little wristwatch with the black leather band and the gold buckle and wondered how on earth he could undo that and take it off without her knowing. It would be impossible.

In the hallway before recess, Tristan said to Lump, "Getting those watches is going to be impossible."

"Nothing is impossible," Lump said.

This, of course, wasn't true. It was something the teachers told the students to encourage them to succeed, to make them realize they could be doctors or heroes or famous baseball players, that they could do anything. But it was odd hearing it coming out of Lump's mouth because, for him, so many things *were* impossible. Being nice, for example. Paying attention in class. Not looking like a giant potato dolt-head.

"Have *you* got any ideas how to do it?" Tristan asked.

Lump stared up at the ceiling. "I'm getting tired of always being the *brains* behind everything."

Tristan stared at Lump's oversized sweaty head. It was hard to imagine him as the brains behind anything. It was hard to imagine that he was even the brains behind himself.

"Just get those watches," Lump said. "Or I'll get *you*. I'll get you like no one's ever been got. Get it?"

After recess Tristan went to his desk and sat and thought, and it was just before lunch that he came up with his daring plan. Part of it had to do with the (very lucky) fact that only one other teacher besides Ms

Barkley wore a watch. Which Tristan had noticed with great relief. There were big clocks in every classroom so no one really needed a watch. There was a clock in the principal's office, in the gym, and even two in the hallways. And part of the plan had to do with how special the watches were to their owners.

At lunchtime Tristan ate his sandwich in two seconds and then walked down the hall looking as innocent and nonchalant as possible. When he saw that no one was looking, he ducked into the washroom that was for the male teachers, no students allowed. He checked quickly to see if anyone was there. One of the stalls had a pair of feet at the bottom so he had to act fast. He picked up the tall white garbage can that everyone threw the paper towels in and he quietly moved it closer to the counter where the sink was. Then he crawled under the counter and hid behind the garbage can. He sat there, his heart beating furiously. After a minute, the man came out of the stall. It was Mr. Feinster, the gym teacher who made them do push-ups on their knuckles and who was almost as mean as Burt Lump.

This was lucky for Tristan, because Mr. Feinster was the other teacher who wore a watch. It was an oversized watch with a million different functions, and one of the functions was to torture all the students in the school when he made them run for twenty (very slow) minutes.

As Mr. Feinster approached the sink, he began to take off his watch. Tristan was counting on this. Mr. Feinster loved his watch. It was the size of a small turtle. He was always looking at it and adjusting it and listening to it. It showed what time it was in twenty-three different countries, which didn't make much sense to Tristan. Unless you were actually *in* that country, who cared what time it was? He was the kind of person, Tristan hoped, who would take off his watch and lay it on the counter and then wash his hands and maybe splash water on his face. When grown-ups washed their hands, he had noticed, they tended to look at the mirror and make faces that they thought made them look more attractive or more serious or more something. They got very close to the mirror, as if there was something they needed to see in their own faces and had to be one centimetre away to do it. They checked

32

to see if there was anything stuck in their teeth, which meant more strange faces. It was just one of the many weird things Tristan decided he wouldn't do when he was grown up. But hopefully today Mr. Feinster would be looking in the mirror, and not down at his watch.

He heard Mr. Feinster lay down his watch and run the water to wash his hands. Without getting out of his hiding spot, Tristan simply reached quickly from behind the garbage can and nimbly plucked the watch and pulled it down and then sat there under the counter, waiting, holding his breath.

The washing sound stopped. Tristan heard the paper towel being ripped from the dispenser, and then being stuffed into the garbage can right next to his head. And then he could almost feel Mr. Feinster's puzzled look. "What the . . ." Tristan heard him say. From under the counter, he saw Mr. Feinster check both his pockets. He stood there for what seemed like two hours and Tristan was sure he was going to get down to see if the watch had fallen on the floor.

But he didn't. He gave out a puzzled sigh, an I-guess-I-left-it-in-the-gym kind of sigh, and left.

Tristan sat under the counter for another five

minutes before he felt it was safe to get out. Then he headed for the female teachers' washroom — a place it would be much worse to be caught in than the men's. Ms Barkley had told the class about her watch, which had been handed down from her mother, who had gotten it from *her* mother, and how valuable it was, and how much it meant to her. This wasn't going to be easy. But he sat there under the women's counter, waiting for her. He was counting on the women eating slower than the men and coming into the washroom later, and this turned out to be more or less true.

After fifteen very nervous minutes, during which most of the women teachers came in and talked about how impossible their students were, Ms Barkley finally arrived. He watched her approach the sink and held his breath and was relieved when he heard the sound of her little gold watch with the black leather band being placed delicately on the counter.

When she was finished washing her hands, she gave a little scream. It wasn't quite a scream, more like a gasp. But he guessed she had seen that the watch wasn't there and was now filled with fear and sadness, and he felt bad about this, but he tried to justify it by imagining how happy she'd be when she got it back. He decided to wait two minutes before sneaking out of the women's washroom.

As Tristan was sitting under the counter in the women's washroom, he was thinking about all his problems. Here he was, his first month in a new school and already he was getting into so much trouble. And just to change the time.

When he thought about it, time was a problem. Every school hour seemed to last a whole day. Each day felt like a week. Sitting in a school where you had no friends and the teacher didn't believe you and the bully came and made you steal things — time went by so slowly it seemed like his whole life had been spent in this school. It had been the longest three weeks of his life, the longest three weeks in the history of the universe.

And it wasn't just school. Home was no better, he thought. His parents didn't have any time for him (or for anything, really). And Bella certainly didn't have time for him. He suddenly realized that his biggest problem wasn't school or Bella or his parents, or even Burt Lump (though he was certainly a big problem): it was *time*. He either had too much of it or not enough, and now it was getting him into trouble. Time, he decided, was his enemy. Time was ruining his life.

Still, no one was more surprised than Tristan when, sitting there under that counter in the women's washroom, he suddenly yelled at the top of his lungs: "I HATE TIME! I WISH IT WAS DEAD! I WANT IT TO END. RIGHT . . . *NOW*!"

He immediately put his hand over his mouth. He couldn't believe he had yelled, and that loud, especially in the women's washroom.

Ms Barkley came bursting in, followed by another teacher.

"Did you hear yelling?" Ms Barkley asked.

"I did," the other teacher said. "It sounded like I ATE SLIME! I WANT TO SUSPEND FLIGHT NOW!"

"I thought it sounded like HIGH RATES ARE FINE! I WISH YOU'D STOP SENDING WHITE COWS!"

After a few minutes, minutes that seemed to Tristan like hours, his heart beating so loudly he couldn't believe they didn't hear it, Ms Barkley finally said, "Well, it seems to have stopped now, whatever it was."

They left, and then the bell rang. Lunchtime was over.

Tristan crept out with both watches in his backpack.

He got back to his desk in Ms Barkley's classroom and very quickly stuffed the watches into Burt Lump's unbelievably messy desk. No one would find them in there. All the kids came in and sat down and Lump immediately opened up his desk and began rustling around in it and Tristan sat there holding his breath, terrified that Lump would find the watches and do something. After a minute of rustling, Lump came up with a small lizard, which he put in his pocket. Tristan let out a (quiet) sigh of relief.

Ms Barkley came in and in her door-slamming voice told them to get out their math books (again).

And then it happened.

At first it was hard to say just *what* happened. There was a curious lull. An emptiness.

It seemed like time had stopped.

It wasn't just the clocks (which Lump *had* changed to read 3:30). It was a feeling that no one could put a name to. The feeling came over the whole class and Tristan could see that Ms Barkley felt it too, whatever it was.

Lump leaned over and whispered to Tristan, "I didn't do it."

Tristan wasn't even sure what "it" was.

It felt to Tristan like something was missing somehow. It reminded him of the time there was nothing good on television and he watched it anyway and he wasn't exactly doing anything since he was barely watching it, but he wasn't really *not* doing anything, either. That was what the day suddenly felt like.

Ms Barkley seemed kind of confused. "What is eight take away eight?" she finally asked. "Eight minus eight, anyone?"

Elaine put up her hand and very quickly said, "Eightminuseight is nothing."

"Yes, it is nothing," Ms Barkley said. "Which is odd when you think about it. I mean, you'd think it would be something, wouldn't you?" Ms Barkley looked kind of dreamy.

Lump put up his hand and said, "Ms Barkley, I'm sorry to interrupt your fascinating lesson, but it's three-thirty." He tried to make his naturally guilty-looking face look innocent, which was pretty much impossible.

"*Three-thirty!* Goodness," Ms Barkley said. "Well, how can that . . ." She looked down at her watch but,

of course, there wasn't one. "Oh. Well. I suppose we should wrap up, class. I don't know where the time went. Tomorrow we'll be looking at the seven times table. Good day, class."

The class all filed out and Burt Lump jogged to catch up with Tristan.

"I didn't do it," Lump said.

"But you *did*," Tristan said, though he supposed they had both done it.

"The clocks, sure, I did that. But *this*," Lump said. "Whatever this is. This big . . . this big nothing. I don't even know what it is. So I couldn't have done it, could I?"

Tristan looked at Lump, with his giant potato body and mean face and extra-sweaty head and, for a moment, it looked like Lump was scared.

"Maybe *you* did it, Blueberry," Lump said, grabbing the front of Tristan's shirt. "If you *did*, you're going to *get* it. Boy, are you going to get it. You'll get it like getting's never been . . . gotten."

Tristan walked home by himself. There was a huge traffic jam on the street, with horns honking and people leaning out of their windows and yelling at each other. There were people standing on their lawns staring up at the sky, as if they were looking for an answer there. But everyone felt it. They all felt the big nothing.

Time had somehow stopped.

And what happens when time stops? How do you even *know* that it's stopped? Well, you feel it. And what it feels like is nothing. Like a big fat nothing that goes on and on. And everyone could feel it, but no one could explain it. Kind of like time itself.

At home Tristan watched the news on television. Every story was about time. It wasn't like there weren't any more hours or minutes. There were. It was just that they didn't seem to mean the same thing anymore. There was an expert on TV trying to explain it.

"Our guest today is Professor Zeno," the interviewer said. "The world's foremost authority on time."

Professor Zeno adjusted his glasses. He was wearing an old suit and had hair like a bird's nest.

"Tell us, Professor," the interviewer said. "What *is* time?"

"Well, we have two kinds of time. One is just the usual — daytime, nighttime, tea time, noon, et cetera.

41

But there is another kind of time that has perplexed philosophers for centuries, from Aristotle to Newton to even Einstein. Time is only noticed by humans. Animals don't acknowledge time, for example. So if no one is around to experience it, does time exist? Does time flow like a river, and does it only go in one direction? Can you travel in time? And if you went back into the past, would you meet yourself? And could you change history?"

"So what's going on right now, Professor?"

Professor Zeno adjusted his glasses again. He stroked his beard and stared into space for what seemed like a very long time.

"I don't actually know," he said.

"You don't know."

"No."

"No clue?"

"None."

"Well, there you have it, folks," the interviewer said. "We seem to be out of time. I think."

The camera stayed focused on the two men, but there was no sound.

Tristan turned off the TV.

Bella got home late because she had been afraid to leave the mall. She thought it might close and never open again.

"Who cares if it closes forever?" Tristan asked.

"Tristan, the mall is the source of all life. Without the mall, we would be naked, hungry and bored."

"But the *mall* is boring."

"Tristan, there are no boring malls. Only boring people. The whole *point* of time is so you know when to open your store in the morning and when to close it at night. And now it's *gone*."

He wanted to tell Bella about the clocks at school and the watches and him yelling that he wanted time to stop and then it did, almost as if by magic, but she wouldn't understand. Tristan couldn't help thinking that maybe Burt Lump was right for probably the first time in his life: maybe it *was* all his fault.

Tristan's parents got home from work even later than usual that night. When they finally arrived it was dark and both Tristan and Bella were asleep.

The Time Keeper

You're probably wondering what happened. Well, it's simple and it's not simple. The simple part is: the Time Keeper quit his job.

You probably think there's just daytime and night-time and playtime and lunchtime. That there are twenty-four hours in a day and sixty minutes in an hour and sixty seconds in a minute. And you'd be right.

But there's another kind of time, isn't there? Professor Zeno was right.

You've probably noticed that when you're standing in front of the class and don't know the answer, two minutes feels like an hour. And maybe you've been on a vacation that seemed to go by in the blink of an eye; before you knew it, you were back in school. Maybe you had a chore to do (raking leaves, mowing the lawn, cleaning your room) that seemed to go on forever.

Well, that didn't happen by accident.

You see, time isn't like, say, money, where it's measured out and every ten-dollar bill is the same as the next ten-dollar bill. There are different kinds of minutes, different sorts of hours. There are different days for different people, for different things. And it's the Time Keeper who makes all those different hours and minutes. If it was just a matter of minutes and hours, there wouldn't be a problem, but it isn't, and so there is.

Why did the Time Keeper quit? Well, he'd been doing it for a very, *very* long time, for one thing. Nobody knows how it got started. It was so long ago.

And he was getting tired of the complaints. People would say, "There just aren't enough hours in the day," or "He simply has too much time on his hands." Over the years there were a lot of complaints. Soon, it was all he heard. It seemed like people spent all their time complaining about time.

People wasted the minutes and resented the seconds. They squandered whole days, and then were angry they were gone. They wanted the days back to do them differently. But no one could do that. When the time was gone, it was gone.

Kids wished they'd spent more time studying for the test. But they only felt that way when they were staring at the test. They hadn't felt that way when they were playing in the park. Back *then*, they weren't wishing they were studying rather than playing. But looking at the test and realizing they didn't know many of the answers, that's when they thought, I should have spent more time on this.

And that's one of the things about time. If you do what you want all the time, you won't be happy. It seems strange, doesn't it? I mean, you're doing what you *want*. How could doing what you *don't* want some of the time make you happier? But it can. And that's why time is so complicated. And why no one has ever really figured it out.

And then the Time Keeper himself started to have doubts about the whole business. And it was while he having doubts that he found himself walking by the school. If any of the kids had glanced out the window, they would have seen someone who looked a bit like a handyman, which is what he was, sort of. The world's oldest handyman. He was tall and lean and his shoulders were a bit stooped. But he didn't look that old, really. Not as old as he was, anyway. And as he walked by the school, he heard that scream, he heard those words: "I HATE TIME! I WISH IT WAS *DEAD!* I WANT IT TO END. RIGHT . . . NOW!"

It was the voice of a young boy. If even boys didn't like time, then who did? Boys who could spend the whole day playing soccer without once thinking of time, the day gone by in a wonderful flash.

Maybe everyone is better off without me, he thought. The Time Keeper walked back to his house with a heavy heart, and with his shoulders a little more stooped.

It was quite a long walk. Not far from the house was a big red barn. This was where he kept his time-making machine. It was gigantic. It filled the whole barn, almost touching the ceiling. It was shiny, mostly made of steel, and it made a loud ticking sound. There were levers and pulleys and sprockets and toggles and safety glass. And it never stopped. The machine was always going, always making time.

All over it, signs clearly marked the buttons for

the different kinds of time it made: **LARGE HOURS** (for reading long books, learning arithmetic, sitting in church, waiting to open presents, etc.), **MEDIUM MINUTES** (for standing in front of the class not knowing the answer, visits to the doctor, talks with aunts you only see once a year, etc.), **SHORT SECONDS** (for wondering where the time has gone), **EXTRA-LONG MINUTES** (for staring at plates of cold vegetables that aren't going to go away by themselves).

The Time Keeper stared long and hard at the machine. He listened to the ticking sound. It was a sound that he had heard most of his life. It was like music to him.

Yet no one appreciated his time. No one ever thanked him for the time they had, they only resented him for the time they didn't have.

There was only one thing to do, he thought: I'll quit.

His hand reached for the button marked **OFF**. For a very long minute it hovered over the button. The Time Keeper thought about all the happy times that had come out of his machine. All the long summer days, the warm hours in front of a fire in winter, the fleeting minutes of a spring day.

He pushed the button.

With a great shudder, and a series of loud coughs, the time-making machine stopped.

There was a silence that hadn't been heard since the beginning of time.

The Big Nothing

When Tristan woke up the next morning, the world had changed.

How could this happen? he wondered. He had stolen two watches (not even really stolen, since they were still at the school in Lump's desk and he was going to give them back), and he had yelled that he hated time. And then it stopped. Was it *his* fault? Was he to blame for all this?

He got dressed and went downstairs for breakfast. His parents were standing up, eating toast.

"Are we late?" his mother asked nervously.

"I think so," his father said. "I think we're very late."

"Or maybe very early," his mother said.

"Or very, *very* late."

"Right."

They finished their toast, kissed Tristan and Bella and left for work. Tristan had a bowl of cereal and then he and Bella walked to the bus stop and Bella didn't even worry about being seen with him. They waited for a while but no bus came and they finally just started walking.

"I hope we're not late," Tristan said.

"Of course, we're late."

"How do you know?"

"I just know. I mean, everything's late."

Maybe, Tristan thought, if I yelled out that I loved time, maybe it would reverse things. He suddenly yelled at the top of his lungs: "I LOVE TIME! I WANT IT TO GO ON FOREVER. I . . . JUST . . . *LOVE . . . IT!*"

Tristan waited expectantly, but nothing happened.

His sister stared at him. "Tristan, you are so weird. No wonder I don't walk with you."

The bus finally pulled up beside them. Bella kept walking, but Tristan got on. Everyone on the bus looked kind of mopey. Except Lump, who looked mopey and mean. He gave Tristan a particularly dark look as he sat down.

"Blueberry," he said. "This, this . . . big nothing. You did it, didn't you? It was you, wasn't it?"

The thing about Lump was, he wasn't very smart, but certain things he kind of understood instinctively. Anything bad, for example. Maybe Tristan was giving off some kind of guilty scent. He had read that dogs could smell fear. Maybe naturally guilty people (and Lump would certainly fall into that group) could smell guilt. And Tristan felt guilty.

"How could it be me?" Tristan said. "I mean, how could a kid stop time? It's not like I have magic powers. I can't just yell, 'I want time to stop!' and it does." Although this is exactly what had happened. He'd yelled and time had stopped. He stared at Lump, trying to look as innocent as possible.

"Stop trying to look innocent, Blueberry."

At school it was chaos. Not many teachers were there, for one thing. Kids were wandering out of their class-rooms and eating their lunches in the hallway because they were worried it was lunchtime. The day just kind of dribbled by and Tristan didn't learn anything and after a while everyone was sent home.

On the bus back home, Lump said, "I don't like this. I don't like it one bit. You know why I don't like it, Blueberry?"

Tristan didn't know, and he didn't care, but that wouldn't stop Lump from telling him.

"My day is busy. My day, Blueberry, is filled with . . ." he paused, searching for the right word, "*purpose*."

It was hard to believe that Lump's day was filled with anything other than confusion and stupidity.

"You think it's easy being a bully, Blueberry? Try it sometime. It's hard. I have a lot of people to see, a lot of people to bully. It's a lot of *work*."

Tristan nodded. He hadn't really given much thought to the problems associated with bullying.

"But now there isn't enough *time* to bully everyone. Maybe there isn't *any* time. All thanks to you. I'll be lucky to get around to half of my customers."

Tristan thought that this might be the only good thing about time having stopped: less bullying.

"And that's where you come in, Blueberry. You're going to help me."

"Help you? Help you what?"

"Help me bully."

"*Help* you bully?"

"That's right. You're going to bully all those people I don't have time to bully."

"But I'd be a *terrible* bully," Tristan said. "Anyway, you can't just decide to be a bully."

"Well, it helps to have natural talent," Lump said. "It's true, I've got a gift."

You have a fat head, a potato body and the brain of a fruit fly, Tristan thought.

"You don't have that gift," Lump said. "But you're the one who got me into this mess and you're the one who's going to get me out of it. Are we clear?"

"But how can I be a bully?" Tristan said. "In order to be a bully, people have to be afraid of you, don't they? And no one's afraid of me."

"They will be, after I make you my deputy. You know in those cowboy movies there's the sheriff and the deputy. Well, you're my deputy."

Tristan couldn't imagine a worse thing. He would now have to go and try to bully people who were bigger than him. A new kid, a *new* new kid at that, going around bullying people in his new school. They would beat him up, and then he'd go back to Lump and tell him what happened and Lump would beat him up for failing to be a good bully. This was an impossible situation. The *worst* impossible situation.

"You start tomorrow," Lump said.

"I can't do it."

"Oh, you can do it. You *will* do it, Blueberry. Because if you don't, I'll *get* you. You'll be so *got* that you won't even believe how gotten you're . . . going to get."

Maybe I can help him with his threats at least, Tristan thought.

"Tomorrow, Deputy Blueberry."

Bully

The night passed (super) slowly. Tristan lay awake thinking how awful the day was going to be, how all other awful days he'd had (and there were lots of them) would be nothing compared to this awful day. This would be the worst day of his life. Not many people know they are going to have the worst day of their life before they even have it. But Tristan did.

At breakfast his father was reading the paper and eating toast. His mother was talking on the phone and eating a granola bar and checking her purse for something.

"I've decided to become a bully," Tristan said.

"Hmm," his father said, still staring at the paper. "Good luck, sport."

"I'll probably beat up a few kids this morning. Take

their lunch money. Maybe throw their hats onto the school roof."

"That's great, dear," his mother said, punching in another number on her phone. "I knew you'd fit in."

"I might steal a few bicycles."

"Bicycles," his father repeated. "Great way to get around. Had a red one when I was a kid."

"The thing is," Tristan said. "I mean, why stop at bicycles? Why not steal the teacher's car? I'll steal it and then drive to Mexico."

"Love Mexico!" his mother said, checking for messages on her phone.

"Maybe get a job as a bandito."

"Hmm," his father said.

"Rob some trains. Live the crazy life of El Bandito."

"Gotta dash," his mother and father said at the same time and they were suddenly gone.

Bella looked at him. "Tristan, you are *so* weird."

The bus arrived late (or felt like it, anyway) and was only half full. But Tristan still felt obliged to sit beside Lump. The ride was, as he had guessed, the first awful stop in his awful day. Lump gave him a list of names scrawled in his terrible handwriting (the worst in the class by far) and Tristan couldn't even read most of it.

"What's this one?" he asked, pointing to some squiggly lines.

"Can't you read, Blueberry?"

The problem, of course, was that Lump couldn't write. But this was the beauty of being a bully. It was always someone else's fault.

"It looks like . . ." Tristan squinted. "Ratmaninsky-winsky."

"It's *Smith*," Lump said. "S. W. O. . . . something H. *Smith*." Lump's spelling was even worse than his writing. "You gotta brush up on your reading skills, Blueberry. Bullies have, like, standards."

Tristan wondered what they could possibly be.

"This is the list of people you have to bully today," Lump said. "Every morning I'll give you a new list."

Tristan took a look at the list. There were eighteen names on it. How would he ever find the time to bully eighteen people?

"This seems like an awfully long list," Tristan said.

"Hard work is rewarded," Lump said. "You may as well start with Smith."

"*Grant* Smith?"

"That's him."

"But he's, I don't know, twice my size. How am I going to bully him?"

"You always look at the negative, Blueberry. It's not how people get ahead in life."

Tristan stared at Lump. At his head, which seemed to have somehow grown even bigger in the night, those beady eyes, the expression of a stegosaurus. And now Lump was giving him career advice.

"I expect results," Lump said.

"What *are* results in the bullying world?" Tristan asked.

"I'll need lunches, lunch money, valuable trading cards and homework assignments done for me. But most of all, and this is the most important thing, Blueberry, I'll need fear."

Well, he already had fear, Tristan thought. Mine. Fear of going around the school bullying people. Tristan had dreaded a lot of things, but not as much as he dreaded this. It was odd that he dreaded bullying even more than he dreaded being bullied.

He saw Grant Smith standing with two of his friends. For all he knew, they were on the list too. But then he couldn't read the list, and he didn't know the names of most of the kids in school anyway and so he had no way of knowing. He sort of sauntered over and then kind of loitered around them until finally (the very tall) Grant Smith said, "You want something?"

Tristan looked up at him. "Um, do you have any cards?"

"Cards?"

"Valuable trading cards."

"Are you nuts? Who *are* you, anyway?"

"How about a lunch? Do you have a lunch?"

"Do I have *cards*? Do I have a *lunch*? Do you have a *brain*?"

The other two laughed and then they went back to talking to each other and Tristan slunk away.

The next name on the list was, he managed to make out, his own — Bloobarry — although it wasn't spelled correctly. Lump expected him to bully himself! How did you even do that? Did he have to threaten himself?

"You have any valuable trading cards, Blueberry?" he asked himself.

"Maybe I do and maybe I don't," he replied.

"Well, give them here."

"Or what?"

"*Or what?* Or you'll *get* it, that's what."

"Get what exactly?"

"Get 'it'."

"What's 'it'?"

"It's what you'll *get* if you don't give me those cards."
Tristan grabbed his own shirt and pulled it up like a
bully would.

"Oh yeah, well, I'm not afraid of *you*."

"Well, you *better* be afraid of me . . ."

"Or what?"

"Or you'll *get* it so completely that there won't be
any more getting to be gotten. By anyone. *Ever.*"

"Oh yeah? Well, you don't scare . . ."

It was then that Tristan noticed Bella and her friends
were standing behind him, watching him bully himself. He stared at them. They stared at him. He took
his hand away from his bunched-up shirt and then
smoothed it a bit.

"Tristan, you are the weirdest brother on the planet
Earth," Bella said, and they all walked away.

No matter how hard he squinted, Tristan couldn't read any of the other names on the list, so it looked like his bullying career had come to an end. He couldn't even bully himself. This must be a new record in the bullying world, he thought. He must officially be the world's worst bully. He wondered if this was something he should be proud of, or if it was just one more thing he wasn't good at.

The morning kind of disappeared, then lunch vanished (if it even was lunch) and the next thing he knew, Tristan was sitting on the half-empty school bus, talking to Lump.

"Let's have it," Lump said.

"Well, the thing you have to understand . . ." Tristan started.

"I'm a bully," Lump said. "I don't have to understand anything."

"The first day didn't go too well."

"Valuable trading cards?"

"No."

"Lunches?"

"Not exactly."

"Money?"

"Not as such."

Lump looked up and sighed. "What about fear, Blueberry? What about the most important thing?"

"There was fear," Tristan said. "Quite a bit, actually." He wouldn't bother telling Lump it was all his own.

"I can only give you one more chance. Tomorrow, you get results. Or I will get you in ways that will get you gotten . . . in ways you won't even *get.*"

When Tristan got back from his first day of bullying, no one was home. He turned on the TV and Lulu Adams's show was on and he sat and watched as she explained how elephants knew it was time to die and when they knew this they started to walk to the secret elephant graveyard.

And this gave him an idea. Maybe time hadn't disappeared for animals, he thought. That's what Professor Zeno had said on TV. And if didn't exist for animals, how could it be gone? Maybe it wasn't really gone. It was just that people couldn't find it. And maybe he could be the person who found it and then he'd bring it back and he'd be a hero and have lots of friends and

Lump wouldn't make him bully people and his mother would have time to take him to the zoo.

The place to start was the zoo. That's where all the animals were. He could take the bus, even though he wasn't supposed to. He knew what bus to take, and he knew where the zoo was, sort of. He got his backpack and took out the school stuff and filled it with things he thought he might need for the trip. He made sandwiches and found two cans of juice and some apples and his global positioning device and other things he thought could be useful.

He left the house and walked to the bus stop and waited for a very long time until a bus finally showed up. No one else was on it. The bus wound through the streets, which were strangely empty.

The bus dropped him off near the zoo gates. He got to the ticket booth, only there was no one in it to take his money. Tristan called out, just to be sure, in case the attendant was on the floor looking for something, or sleeping maybe. "Hello," he called out. "Hello. Anyone?"

No one answered, so Tristan just went in through the open gate. He walked down a path that was marked with painted-on animal tracks — blue lion paw prints. They led to the Africa House and Tristan walked in and felt a comforting warmth, like actually being in the jungle.

But it was also quite dark. He supposed jungles *were* dark. The trees were so thick the sun couldn't get through. Still, he wasn't sure he wanted to be somewhere dark on his own. But it occurred to him that he could get as close as he wanted to any of the cages. He wouldn't be crowded out by bigger boys who pushed him aside so they could tap on the glass right beside the sign that said, PLEASE DO NOT TAP ON THE GLASS.

The python was lying in a thick pile and Tristan moved close to the glass and stared at it. "Where do you think time went?" he asked the python. The python looked up at Tristan and it seemed like there was a smile on his face, except everyone knows that snakes don't smile.

Tristan went to the cobra next and then looked at all the lizards and then walked through the extra-dark tunnel where the bats were. There was a fish tank that had a thousand fish in it, blue and yellow and green

darting in one direction then another, like they all had exactly the same idea at exactly the same time. It didn't seem like the animals were behaving any differently. They didn't seem to miss time.

He spent so long in the Africa House that when he came out it was almost as dark outside as it had been inside.

He started to walk, and then he started to run.

Bella

One of the things that Bella liked about the mall was that it was filled with people. All kinds of people. People she could look at and think, "I'm glad I'm not *that* person." Which she did quite a bit.

Except there weren't that many people and they were kind of straggling through the stores. Some of the stores weren't even open. Their windows were dark and that was kind of depressing. And she was supposed to meet Boink and Sarah except they didn't show up, or they had shown up but at the wrong time. It seemed like *all* time was wrong somehow. Anyway, here she was in the mall, by herself, and it occurred to her that she wasn't having any fun.

She went into a store and tried on a pair of jeans, but it didn't help. She looked at the movies in the megaplex. Usually they had the times of each movie posted outside. Now there was just a sign that read, WHENEVER.

She walked around for an hour. She could see it was starting to get dark outside and she thought she'd better be getting home.

Outside, she stood at the bus stop and waited for a while, feeling a bit nervous. There wasn't anyone around. A bus came and she got on and she was the only person on it.

When she got home, the house was dark. She used her key to let herself in.

"Mom?" She called out. "Dad?" She walked through the house calling out their names. "*Tristan*?" she tried.

But there was no answer. The house was empty.

On the kitchen counter there was a note.

"Bella," it read. "We're at work. Take care of your brother. Mom & Dad. PS: Take good care of him."

Take care of your brother? Where *was* her brother? Tristan was always kind of a nuisance, but now he was a big nuisance. Plus he was kind of young to be out somewhere by himself. Where *was* he?

Bella sat down to think. If she didn't find him, her

parents would kill her. They would take away her mall privileges. Or worse, if there was anything worse.

Where could he be? She went up to his room, as if there might be some clues there. On his desk there was a model of a pirate ship and a picture of an alien he had drawn. Maybe he joined a gang of pirates, she thought. Or he was kidnapped by aliens. How could *that* be her fault?

On the floor was a large drawing of a neighbourhood that looked like their own neighbourhood. Except at each house there was a photograph of an animal that had been cut out and pasted onto the house.

Bella stared at it for a moment.

Of course, she thought. Where else would he be? He's at the zoo.

She raced out of the house and stood at the bus stop for what seemed like an impossibly long time until a bus finally came and she got on.

"Are you going to the zoo?" she asked the driver.

"I can take you anywhere you want," the driver said. "It's not like there's anyone else taking the bus."

Bella looked around. It was true. The bus was empty.

They drove to the zoo, and the driver let her out.

"You sure you want to go to the zoo?" she asked. "I mean, it's a little late."

"I don't *want* to go to the zoo," Bella said. "I *have* to go."

She got off and the bus drove away and Bella approached the gates. She pushed against them but they were locked.

"Tristan," she yelled. "Tristaaaaaaan." She walked partway around the zoo fence, yelling his name. She peered in, but there didn't appear to be anyone in there. What if he's been eaten by a tiger? she thought. Or a polar bear. Animals were always escaping from zoos and eating things. You heard it on the news all the time.

She started walking. Maybe Tristan was on his way home. She hoped so.

She walked for a while and realized she didn't actually know where she was. And there probably weren't any more buses running. It was dark and a cloud moved to cover the light of the moon.

Well, this is just great, she thought. Just perfect.

She kept walking. What else was there to do?

The Journey

After he left the zoo, Tristan hurried to the bus stop and stood there and waited. He waited and waited, but the bus didn't come. He ran until he found another bus stop. It was getting darker, and Tristan was getting a bit scared. Not *actually* scared, he told himself. Concerned, maybe. But it got darker and he got more concerned.

He saw someone walking toward him, and he got even *more* concerned. The person got closer and it seemed like a big person. Maybe a monster, he thought. Maybe a monster that hung around bus stops and ate people when the bus didn't come, which made sense when you thought about it.

"The bus didn't come?" the monster asked.

Tristan recognized that voice.

It was Bella. His sister. He was so happy to hear her voice he almost burst into tears.

But he didn't.

"Bella!" he yelled. He couldn't remember the last time he had been happy to see her. Maybe there hadn't been a last time. But he was happy to see her now.

"Tristan, what are you *doing* here? We're in the middle of . . ." She looked around. "We're in the middle of nowhere."

"I went to the zoo," he said, speaking very quickly. "I was waiting for a bus except there wasn't one and there was no one in the zoo and I stayed in the Africa House too long and time is gone and it's all my fault because Burt Lump changed the clocks and made me steal the watches and he's a bully and he looks like a big potato well actually two big potatoes . . ."

"It's okay," Bella said staring at her brother. "It's okay, Tristan. We'll just get a bus and go home." She looked into the gloomy night. "Mom and Dad are going to kill us."

They stood there together and waited. And waited. There wasn't any bus. In fact, there wasn't any anything. No cars drove by, no people. Nothing. It was a bit creepy. Also, it was very dark.

"I guess we'll have to walk," Bella said.

They started to walk.

Tristan heard noises: an owl, a dog and a few sounds he couldn't identify. They walked until they were too tired to walk anymore. Clouds had moved in and it was completely dark now and it was clear they were lost. Tristan reached for Bella's hand and held it. They saw a very large barn in a field, and they crossed over and Bella knocked on the side door. She knocked louder and called out, "Is anyone home?" But no one answered. Bella tried the door handle. It was unlocked, and they both slipped inside. It was so dark they could hardly see their hands.

"What should we do?" Tristan asked.

"There isn't much we can do in the dark," she said. "Let's just go to sleep and figure it out in the morning."

They curled up on the floor.

"Who's Burt Lump?" Bella asked.

But Tristan was already asleep.

The Big Machine

Tristan woke up the next morning with the sun shining on his face. There were big windows in the ceiling of the barn, and the sun had turned everything a brilliant yellow. The light bounced off the biggest machine Tristan had ever seen in his life. It almost reached the ceiling. It was shiny, and it was silent. He looked at the machine for a while. I wonder what it makes, he thought. Bella woke up and stared at the machine too. They looked around for signs of activity, but no one was there.

"I'm starving," she said.

Tristan looked in his backpack and pulled out two sandwiches and two apple juices and gave one of each to his sister.

"Thanks, Tristan," Bella said, hungrily eating the sandwich. "You brought sandwiches. That was smart."

It was the first time ever that she had said he'd done something smart, and Tristan was surprised. Usually, she told him that whatever he was doing was dumb. Even if he wasn't doing anything.

They went outside and saw a man sleeping in a hammock. He was kind of slouchy looking, though it's hard not to be slouchy in a hammock.

"Is that your machine?" Tristan asked him.

The man opened one eye and looked at Tristan and Bella.

"No," he said, closing the eye.

"Whose is it?" Tristan asked.

He opened the other eye. "It's the Time Keeper's."

"What does it make?"

The man opened both eyes and looked up. "What does it make? What does it *make?* It makes time, of course."

"This is where all the time is made?" Tristan said.

"Not anymore," he said. "The Time Keeper quit. Time is now a thing of the past."

Tristan and Bella looked at each other.

"Well, maybe we could start it up," offered Tristan. "We could make some time."

"Only the Time Keeper knows how to make time. What's your name, anyway?"

"Tristan. This is my sister Bella. What's your name?"

"Idle. I was his assistant."

"Then you must know something about how it works."

"It's all very complicated." Idle stared up at the sky.

"But we *need* time," Tristan said. "Look at what's happening. Everyone is late, or early — and scared or lost or worried or . . ."

"Not me," Idle said. "I'm not worried."

"But don't you want to find him? Don't you want your job back?"

"I couldn't be happier," said Idle, who was the laziest assistant in the world, and who didn't want any job back. "I've got nothing but time on my hands."

"But you *don't*," Bella said. "You don't have *anything* on your hands."

Idle mulled this over. Then his eyebrows shot up. He stared and then suddenly sat upright. This was something he hadn't considered. "You're saying . . ."

"I'm saying you can't waste time," Bella said, "if there's no time to waste."

"We have to go and find him," Tristan said.

"Good luck," Idle said, and closed his eyes.

Tristan turned to his sister. "It's my fault," he said. "So I have to find him."

"Tristan, I highly doubt that this could all be *your* fault."

He explained about Burt Lump and the clocks and stealing the watches and then yelling how he hated time. And then time stopping. "Don't you see, it's all my fault and I have to save time or Mom and Dad will spend their whole lives at work and the whole world will go crazy and Lump will *get* me and . . ."

"Okay, okay," Bella said. Her brother's life was a mystery to her. "Well, if we're going to find this guy, we need to know something about him."

They looked at Idle, who had drifted off to sleep again. Bella nudged him so he spun around, fell out of the hammock onto the ground, and woke up.

"Idle," she said, "we need some information."

To the Sea

Tristan and Bella set off down the road, walking briskly.

The first question, of course, was: where did he go? What does the Time Keeper do when he quits? Tristan had seen detectives on TV. They always had a description of the person they were looking for, and they also had clues.

Idle had told them that the Time Keeper was old. Really old. Not forty or fifty, more like twelve hundred. He said he didn't have any hobbies, that all he did was work, which is all most grown-ups seemed to do. It wasn't much to go on.

"He did say one other thing," Tristan said, continuing that thought.

"Who did?" Bella said.

"Idle. Remember? He said that the Time Keeper had

been thinking about taking a vacation, that he wanted to go to the sea."

Bella pondered this.

"How far is the sea from here?" Tristan asked.

"Well, it wouldn't be that far if we could take a train, or a plane, or a car. But we can't, really. It's pretty far to walk. But we could do it, I guess. If we had to."

They were both thinking the same thing: they had to.

They walked along the road. Along the edge of their town there were some farms and then after that, there were some woods, and beyond that, there were hills. That much they knew. And they had a map, sort of. Tristan took out his global positioning device, the one that up to this point in his life had shown him that he was in pretty much the same place all the time.

"Does that thing work?" Bella asked.

"I don't know. I've only tried it in places where I know where I am."

According to his GPS they should be going straight, which led into a forest.

In the forest, Tristan could see large patches of blue

sky through the tops of the trees. Walking among the trees was very pleasant. The birds sang and the sun filtered through the leaves onto the path. They walked for a while and Tristan thought about all the things he'd left behind. He wondered what his mom and dad were doing. He wondered what Lump was doing. Then the woods ended and so did the path, and they were staring out to blue-coloured hills that formed an uneven line against the sky.

"Where's the sea?" Tristan asked.

"On the other side of those hills," Bella said. "I think."

The grass was high here and it tickled Tristan as he walked. After what seemed like a long time, they saw a town sitting against the hills. From a distance, it looked like their town. From a distance, most towns looked alike.

"Maybe the Time Keeper is there," Tristan said hopefully. "Maybe he just wanted to go on a vacation and he's stopping at this town on his way to the sea."

"I hope so," Bella said.

They walked into the town. There were houses and schools and a few people strolling along the sidewalks. It seemed like a nice normal town.

But then, they all do, don't they? They look normal for a while until you find out just how not-normal they are. And Tristan was already getting the feeling that this was a not-normal town. But not many things *were* normal, now that time had disappeared. How weird will it get? Tristan wondered.

Pretty weird, as it turned out.

He saw a woman walking down the street, smiling a big smile that showed a lot of big white teeth. "You look fabulous," the woman said. "Really, you do. I'm not just saying that."

Tristan wondered who she was talking to. She was all by herself. He noticed that she wore an odd hat with a metal rod sticking out of it, and something hanging from the rod. "Have you done something different?" the woman asked. "I mean you *really* look great." When she got closer, Tristan saw that the square shape hanging from the rod was, in fact, a mirror. The woman was talking to the mirror. She was talking to herself.

Tristan walked up to her. "Excuse me," he said, "but have you seen the Time Keeper?"

"The Time Keeper? The one who makes time?"

Tristan nodded.

"He is the *last* person I want to see."

"Why don't you want to see him?"

"Because as long as he's gone then I won't get any older," she said. And then she marched on past them.

"Do you think that's true?" Tristan asked Bella. "That no one will get any older?"

"I don't know," Bella said. "It would be weird to be the same age your whole life. I mean it sort of defeats the purpose."

Tristan thought about being the same age. Maybe this age, the age he was right now, wasn't the ideal age to be all his life. He would never be able to drive a car for one thing. There were shelves he'd never be able to reach. Movies he couldn't go to. And what about Bella? A whole life spent in the mall.

They kept walking and came to a park. There was a group of guys playing dodge ball and Tristan stopped to watch them. It looked like fun. It looked like any game of dodge ball, but it wasn't boys who were playing, it was men who were his dad's age. Except they didn't sound like they were his dad's age.

"I got you, Dwayne."

"Did not."

"Did too."

"*Not.*"

"*Too.*"

"You're a stupidhead," Dwayne said.

"I know what *you* are but what am *I*?"

"Shut up."

"*You* shut up."

"Make me."

The other man looked at him, and finally said, "I'm taking my ball and going home."

He picked up the ball and started to walk out of the park.

"Who's a big baby?" Dwayne yelled.

"Am not a baby," replied the man with the ball.

"Are too."

"*Not.*"

"Babybabybabybaby."

Tristan and Bella watched the man with the ball walk away. The other men lay down on the grass and stared at the sky and pointed to clouds that were shaped like different things.

"See that one," one of the men said, pointing, "it looks like a camel."

"*Totally* like a camel," another said.

Tristan and Bella resumed walking. "Why are those men acting like they're five years old, I wonder," Bella said.

"Maybe they think that with no time, they can be kids again," Tristan said.

"Speaking of kids," Bella said. "We haven't seen many." Actually, they hadn't seen any. They looked around. There were a few other adults, some of them behaving like kids, but no actual kids.

"I wonder where they are," Tristan said. They walked past stores, most of which were empty. The odd car went by, but the town felt . . . what was that word that grown-ups always used? Irresponsible. The town felt irresponsible. Tristan wondered if it was even possible for a town to be irresponsible, but this one felt like it was.

He was thinking they should probably leave this crazy place when he heard something he hadn't heard since they'd got to the town. It was the sound of a child's voice.

She was singing.

He and Bella stopped and listened to the song.

Where are my minutes?
They've been gone all day
They've just disappeared,
Did they all lose their way?

Did they go shopping?
Did they fly off to Spain?
Are they lost in the mall
Or stuck in the rain?

Are they off exploring?
Did they all join a band?
Have they gone into business
With a lemonade stand?

I don't understand it,
They should've been here —
Are they eating spaghetti
And drinking root beer?

Do they like someone better?
Are we no longer friends?
I sit and I wonder
When will it end?

Tristan and Bella were standing in front of a small house with a fence. On a small patch of grass was a girl, the one who had been singing. She was playing with two dolls.

"Hello," Bella said. "Who are you?"

"Phoebe," the girl said.

There were other kids too, sitting on the lawn with their action figures and bicycles and stuffed animals, boys and girls with dirty faces.

"Are your parents here?" Bella asked, looking at all the kids.

"Not exactly," Phoebe said. "The grown-ups are too busy being kids and taking care of themselves."

"You make your own lunches? You make dinner?" Bella asked. "You put yourselves to bed?"

"We make peanut butter and jam sandwiches, we play all day and go to bed really really late," Phoebe said. "It was fun at first. Now it's not as much fun. It was better when there were grown-ups and kids, instead of everyone being sort of a grown-up and sort of a kid."

"Why do the grown-ups think they're kids?" Bella asked.

"When time stopped, they all thought they wouldn't get any older," Phoebe said. "And now they think they're kids, sort of. Well, they're not exactly kids, but they're not exactly grown-ups."

"I saw a woman talking to a mirror attached to her hat," Bella said.

"That's my Aunt Ruth," Pheobe said. "She thinks if she's always looking at herself then time can't sneak up on her and make her older."

Bella thought this was the saddest thing. She looked at the kids, with their unwashed clothes and dirty faces. If there was a mall around here, she thought, I'd take them all there and get them some new clothes. Except there wasn't a mall.

"Okay," Bella said. "The first thing we need to do is get some clean clothes."

She went inside the house, which was a mess, and found some sheets and towels and came outside and told all the kids to take off their clothes and put on the towels and sheets. Then she took all their dirty clothes and put them in the washing machine and showed Phoebe how it worked.

Tristan pulled some weeds and cut the grass, and Bella got some of the older kids to help her clean the house. She made them all macaroni and cheese and they sat in their towels and sheets and ate it happily. By the time their clothes were dry, Tristan had finished mowing the lawn.

The house was clean, there was a lawn to play on and they were wearing clean clothes. I suppose that's all we can do, Bella thought. She and Tristan waved goodbye to them and headed down the street.

"I don't think we're going to find the Time Keeper here," Bella said.

No, Tristan thought. This wouldn't be the place he'd want to go if he was on vacation.

They walked out of town along the road. There weren't any cars. Tristan found the road on his GPS and figured out where they were.

"It looks like there's a short cut if we go through a big forest," Tristan said.

"I think we should stick to the road," Bella said.

"I don't think we have time to stick to the road."

"I don't know. I mean a big forest is . . ." Bella didn't want to say it was scary or anything, because it would just get Tristan scared. And maybe it would get her scared, but she didn't want to admit that she might be scared. So they went into the big forest.

It was pleasant in the forest. It was pleasant if you weren't thinking that something bad could be living there. If you weren't thinking about bears, for example. Which is what Bella was thinking about.

She listened carefully for bears. And then she heard one. Except it seemed to be playing a guitar.

"Do you hear that?" Tristan said.

"It's someone playing a guitar and singing."

Tristan listened to the slightly whiny voice. He wasn't much of a singer.

"Let's go see," Bella said, walking toward the sound. Tristan followed his sister.

They saw some people sitting around a campfire. Seven of them. Some of them were singing.

"We are the moon, we are the stars, we left our heads on the planet Mars . . ."

Bella and Tristan stopped a few metres away. The singers stopped singing and all seven turned to look at them.

"Whoa, little dudes of the forest," one of them said.

"Hi," Bella said.

Tristan stared at them. All of them had long grey hair and T-shirts with pictures of bands on them. They were all older than his dad.

"Welcome to our part of the forest, man," one of them said. "What brings you here?"

"We're looking for the Time Keeper," Bella said.

"Have you seen him?" Tristan asked.

"The Time Keeper? The dude who makes time? No way, man. That is so uncool."

"But everyone needs time," Tristan said.

"*We* don't need time, man," said the singer, who said his name was Wavy. He introduced the other six: Creaky, Shaky, Wacky, Groovy, Dopey and Doc.

"It's always the same time, if you want it to be," Doc said.

"Well," Bella said, "*Technically*, that isn't exactly how it . . ."

"We control time, it doesn't control us, man," Groovy said.

"What time *is* it, then?" Tristan asked.

"It's . . . like . . . um . . ." Groovy was counting on his fingers. "It's 1969."

Tristan and Bella stared at them.

"But you know it's not *actually* 1969," Bella said.

"It is if we say it is," Dopey said.

"And we say it is," Groovy added.

"Anyway, it doesn't really matter what year it is, because the Time Keeper quit," Bella said. "He isn't making any more time. So maybe it actually *is* 1969."

"He *quit?*" Shaky said. "You're saying that time is now a thing of the past? Man, that is so freaky."

"Super freaky," Groovy said.

"The super-freakiest," said Doc.

"Do you want to help us find him?" Tristan said.

All seven stared at him. "No way," Groovy said. "That is one dude I do *not* want to find."

"Time . . ." Doc said. "Who needs it?"

"Everyone does," Tristan said. "Don't you see?" But Tristan could see that they didn't see. "Without it, where would we be?"

"Right here," Dopey said, dopily.

Bella nudged Tristan. "Well, we should probably be going. It was nice to meet all of you."

They waved goodbye and headed deeper into the forest.

Behind them, they could hear another song. "Oh, Time is an idiot, it stumbles along; yeah, Time is a pinhead, it works out all wrong . . ."

Tristan and Bella walked farther into the trees and pretty soon they couldn't hear them anymore, which was a relief.

"Why is it," Tristan asked, "that grown-ups have so many problems with time? I mean, that woman with the mirror, and those guys playing dodge ball who didn't even think they *were* grown-ups. And then these guys in the forest, who are stuck in the past. And then Mom and Dad, who never seem to *have* any time. Why can't they figure it out?"

"Maybe it's harder than it looks," Bella said.

Retirement

You might be asking yourself: just where *was* the Time Keeper? What would he do? Well, he was asking himself that same question. He had worked all his very, *very* long life and now he had stopped and he didn't know what to do. What did retired people do? They sat on porches. They played with their grandchildren. They complained about things.

And they golfed.

And that is how the Time Keeper found himself playing what seemed like the longest game of golf in the world. How long? Who knows. But it seemed to go on forever.

He was standing in the middle of a huge green golf course that stretched on and on. He was playing with a man with a huge white beard, wearing red shorts.

"What's the score, Nick?" the Time Keeper asked.

"Let's see." Nick ran his finger down a piece of paper he was holding, a score sheet that trailed after them for twenty metres. "*You* . . . have . . . four million and sixty-three. And I, uhmm, I have four million sixty-*two*. I'm winning."

The Time Keeper lined up his ball, then he sort of wiggled his behind, like he was backing into a prickle bush, then he pulled the golf club back and swung. There wasn't a thwacking sound, but more of a *dink*. The ball travelled a couple of metres.

"Nice shot," said Nick.

Balls had gotten lost in the woods, balls had disappeared down gopher holes, balls had landed in water and sand. He wondered if he and Nick were going around in circles. Some of the trees he hit seemed familiar, as if he had hit them before. And if they were going in circles, why wasn't he getting any better at the game? It occurred to him that he hated golf.

He lined up his ball and stared down at it. He concentrated on hitting the ball perfectly. He imagined it flying upward in a cool perfect arc and slowly descending and landing right by the hole and then slowly rolling in. He raised his club and drew it back and, when

he swung, he hit the ball *perfectly*, just like he had imagined. And it *was* travelling in a cool perfect arc and was headed right for the hole.

A huge eagle swooped down and grabbed the ball out of the air and flew away with it.

The Time Keeper watched the eagle fly west until it was a tiny speck and it disappeared.

"You don't see that every day," Nick said.

"I have golfed enough," the Time Keeper said.

"You can never golf enough. Anyway, you can't quit now. The game isn't finished."

"But I am," the Time Keeper said. He left his golf bag right there and began walking. He didn't know where he was going. It would take him a while just to get off the huge golf course.

Nick yelled after him, "I know one guy who isn't getting anything in his Christmas stocking this year."

While the Time Keeper knew he didn't want to play any more golf, he wasn't sure what he wanted to do. Maybe, he thought, I should go on a vacation. What did people *do* on vacations? He'd never been on one, really. At least, he couldn't remember one. Childhood was such a long, long time ago. Did they even have holidays back then? he wondered. Hadn't they gone to the sea? Maybe he should rent a nice little cottage and watch the sunset and go to sleep to the sound of the waves softly lapping at the shore.

He wondered what Idle was doing. While he was maybe the laziest assistant in the world, the Time Keeper missed him.

He missed his job too. He had thought it was such an important job. Everyone's life was made up of moments, one after the other. But only some moments were important, only some were memorable. You had to be careful. It wasn't easy making time for everybody in the world. It was a science, but it was also an art.

The Time Keeper's trudge was slow. His footsteps were heavy. He missed *time*. Where would he go? What would he do? Had all his work been for nothing? A life spent making something that no one wanted? What a terrible thought. All that time spent making time, but never making any for himself. Had it all been a waste? What else could he have done? What else *should* he have done? These thoughts weighed heavily on him. They weighed so heavily that he didn't notice he was off the golf course. So heavily that he didn't notice the trap.

He stepped into what looked like a small, not-at-all dangerous pile of leaves. But the leaves were covering a circle of rope, and at the other end of that rope were four pairs of large hairy hands, getting ready to yank as hard as they could. When his foot entered the circle, the rope tightened around his ankle and suddenly, *whoosh*, he was hanging upside down, bobbing at the end of the bouncy rope.

As he bounced slightly, he could see four upside-down figures come out of the trees, curious-looking people with clocks strapped to them, or tied on with string, and watches on their arms. Not just one watch, but *lots* of watches. When he had finished bouncing, and the upside-down faces of his captors came into focus, the Time Keeper said, "And who might you be?"

"We are the ferocious Time Bandits," one of them said. "We are feared throughout the world." He was thick and hairy with a nose like a turnip. His breath smelled like a wet dog. His hair was spiky and dark. "You've heard of us?" he said to the Time Keeper hopefully.

"No," the Time Keeper said.

"You've heard of *time?*" the man said.

"Yes," the Time Keeper said. "I've heard of it."

"And you've heard of bandits?"

"I suppose."

"Aha! Then you *have* heard of us."

The Time Keeper's face was getting red from hanging upside down, and the men slowly lowered him to the ground.

He stood up and brushed off the leaves and looked at his captors right side up. Their clothes were dirty, and they had hair growing out of their ears. And all those clocks and watches strapped to them, not just on their arms, but on their legs too.

"You steal watches," the Time Keeper said.

"Watches, clocks. But eventually," dog breath said, "we are going to steal time *itself*. All of it."

"Really," the Time Keeper said. "And what would you do with it?"

"Our plan . . ." he began.

"Our *evil* plan . . ." one of the other goons corrected.

"Our evil plan is, we're going to sell it to people. For millions and *millions. Billions!*"

"I see," the Time Keeper said. "How can you steal something you can't see?"

"Well, we'll . . . What we're going to do is . . . It's very complicated. Our leader is figuring that part out."

"And who is your leader?"

"The incredible, the fabulous, the wicked, wicked Thief of Time," dog breath said, as if he was introducing him on stage. "He's very famous."

"The Thief of Time. And you're taking me to see him, are you? That's generally how these things work."

"We are," dog breath said. He turned to the others. "On to the Thief of Time!" he announced. "Let's march!"

As they began to march (and not very well, it must be said), dog breath looked up at his prisoner. "And who are you?" he asked.

"I'm the Time Keeper."

Dog breath and the others stopped marching, crashing into one another like hairy dominoes. They stared at the Time Keeper with their mouths open, too stunned to say a word.

Through the Forest

Bella and Tristan were following a small path that wound through the forest, which seemed to go on forever.

"Do you think this path leads to the sea?" Bella asked.

"I don't know," Tristan said, looking at his GPS. "It might be the only path. But even if we find him, how are we going to convince him to come back and make time?"

Bella hadn't thought of this. It was true. What if the Time Keeper didn't want to go back to work? What if he was happy on vacation and just wanted to relax?

"Maybe he could tell us how the machine works and where all the minutes and hours go and then *we* could do the job," Tristan said.

"I don't know," Bella said.

"But what *is* time, anyway? Why are the minutes so long when you're waiting for your favourite TV show to start, but the minutes in the actual show are short?"

Bella had noticed the same thing, but she didn't have an answer. "We'll have to ask the Time Keeper," she said. "If anyone can explain the mysteries of time, it would be him."

Bella was enjoying the walk. The air was cool and smelled like pine. She hadn't spent so much time outdoors since, well, since ever. She'd never spent so much time outdoors. But she could see now why people did. The forest was weirdly comforting. The light was lovely. The earth felt good under her feet.

They walked until the sun was low.

"I wonder who lives out here," Tristan said.

"No one," said Bella. "Obviously."

"Then why is there a path here?" Tristan asked. "I mean *someone* must live here . . ." He stopped and looked around. "The path!" he suddenly yelled.

"What?" Bella asked.

"Where did it go?" Tristan asked.

Bella had been so busy thinking about how nice the outdoors was and how maybe they should think about building an outdoor mall where all the stores were outside, that she didn't notice that they had lost the path. Or the path had lost them. At any rate, it was gone. The other thing that was gone was the sun. It was getting dark.

They stood there and it very quickly became very dark. Then a noise came out of the darkness, a kind of . . . crunching noise.

"What was that?" Tristan asked.

They waited to hear the sound again. But it was quiet.

Tristan held his breath. Until he had to let it out in a loud gasp.

They heard it again. Only this time it was louder. And it certainly sounded crunchy.

"What if that's the sound of crunching bones?" Tristan whispered. "What if those are people's bones being crunched as they're being eaten by a giant people-eating monster?"

"Why would there be a people-eating monster in a place where there are no people?" Bella whispered. "It doesn't make sense."

"Maybe the *reason* there's no people is that the monster *ate* them all," Tristan said. "He might be chewing the last one right now. Maybe this used to be a huge city, a whole *civilization*, and now it's gone."

The two of them stood in the darkness, waiting for the sound, afraid they would hear it and just as afraid they wouldn't hear it.

"The thing about sound," Bella whispered sensibly, "is that it isn't the sound *itself* that's scary. It's not knowing what the sound is. So you think the worst. You think it's a monster when maybe it's a — I don't know — a cow walking over dry twigs making crackling noises. Or a machine crushing things, or . . ."

"Or a big people-eating monster," Tristan said, pointing to what looked to be a big monster.

They froze. Then the monster spoke. Only it wasn't really speaking. It was more like crunching.

"Ack," Tristan said.

"Who are *you*?" the monster said. Except it sounded like he was saying "Bluer Yug."

"What *crunch* are *crunch* you doing *crunch crunch* out here?"

"We're looking for the Time Keeper," Bella said.

"Who isn't?" the monster said, moving toward them slowly.

As he got closer, Bella could see that he wasn't very monstrous. He was wearing a green uniform. He looked sort of like a policeman and he was holding the biggest bag of potato chips that she had ever seen. It was open.

"I eat chips when I'm nervous," the man said. "I'm pretty nervous."

Bella introduced herself and Tristan.

"Mr. Hapstead," the man said, "Call me Hap. I'm the park ranger."

"Park ranger?" Tristan asked.

"This is a National Park. I take care of it. Sort of."

"Why are you so nervous, Hap?" Bella asked.

"I'm afraid of that terrible, terrible thief," he said.

"Who?" Bella asked.

"The Thief of Time." Hap suddenly began eating chips by the fistful.

"What does he look like?"

"Kind of small and terrible and he goes around stealing everyone's watches and clocks. I saw him coming and I hid behind a rock and waited for him to go by."

"Which way did the Thief go?" Tristan asked.

Hap pointed sort of in the direction they'd come from, his mouth full of chips.

"I think we should go that way too," Tristan said.

"Do we really want to run into the terrible Thief of Time?" Bella asked.

"Well," Tristan said, "his job is stealing time. But there isn't any to steal. So now he could be looking for the Time Keeper to force him to make some more."

"If he has him, you'll never be able to rescue him," Hap said. "The Thief has all these goons. Time Bandits."

"Well, we're not going to do any rescuing now, in the middle of the night," Bella said. "Let's get some sleep and we'll figure it out in the morning."

Hapstead said they could sleep in the ranger's cabin, which wasn't far. There was a room with bunk beds and Tristan and Bella collapsed on them without even arguing about who was going to get the top bunk.

When they woke up, Bella noticed for the first time that she had been wearing the same clothes for what seemed like forever, certainly the longest time she'd ever wore the same clothes, and for some reason it didn't bother her. Hap made them pancakes and warned them about the Thief of Time.

"Be careful around that terrible guy," Hapstead said. "Be *very* careful."

The Thief
of Time

The Time Keeper stared at the Thief of Time. One thing you could say about him was that he was on the small side. Another thing you could say was that he was unpleasant looking. His teeth were green and a bit furry. His eyes looked like raisins stuck in his pudding face. On his head was a clock that had been made into a hat, though not too successfully. His hands were small and damp-looking and they were softly petting a grey rat. This was the Thief of Time.

"So you are the great Time Keeper," the Thief said with glee. "You make time." His voice sounded like a hinge that needed oil.

"Yes and no," the Time Keeper answered.

The Time Bandits huddled nearby, their dog breath coming out like a horrible fog.

"Well, well, well. This is my lucky day. My *luckiest* day. Do you know what I do?" he asked squeakily.

"I hear you're a thief. That you steal time."

"Yes, yes. You've heard of me. Good, good."

Actually the Time Keeper hadn't heard of him before today, but he felt it was better not to say so. "How much have you stolen so far?" he asked.

The Thief of Time smiled, a truly terrible smile, the kind where you know he looked better *not* smiling. "So far, it's just watches and clocks. But once I figure out how to steal time *itself,* I will rule the world."

"I see," the Time Keeper said. He thought about telling the Thief that stealing was wrong. But the Thief was the kind of person who already knew it was wrong. That's why he did it. If it was *right,* he'd quit doing it.

"Let me tell you something," the Thief began. "You've really made a mess of this whole time thing. People don't want to spend what seems like an hour staring at cold porridge. And they want the sunsets to last longer. They want birthday parties to go on for *days.* Well, the kids do anyway. Maybe you're just too old for the job and you're getting confused. I don't know." The Thief stared upward, furiously stroking his pet rat. "People would be better off with *me*. *I'll* make their lives better. The ones who have money, anyway. *You've* made their lives worse. Once I start selling time to them, they can do whatever they want."

"In my experience," the Time Keeper said, "it's not always a good idea to give people what they want. Is it a good idea to give a child forty-three ice cream cones because he wants them? Does it make sense to give a girl two hundred dolls because she wants them? If everyone got what they wanted, the world would be in a terrible state."

"The world *is* in a terrible state," the Thief said. "But once you start making me some *time*, things will be better. Guard!" he shouted. "Escort Mr. Time here to the dungeon."

The guard who shuffled forward was the turnip-nosed, dog-breath man who had captured the Time Keeper.

"Take him away, Blunt," the Thief said.

"Move along," Blunt said to the Time Keeper, prodding him with a stick.

The Clue

When Tristan and Bella finished their pancakes, they set off into the forest in the direction the ranger had pointed.

"I think we're heading back toward home," Tristan said, looking at his not-entirely-reliable GPS.

Before long, they found a path and at the side of it, Tristan saw something shiny, glinting in the sun. He walked over to have a look.

"What is it?" Bella asked.

Tristan held it up. "It's a watch." He examined it carefully. On the face of the watch were the initials TK. "Maybe this is the Time Keeper's watch, Bella. See the initials?"

"If it *is* his watch, then it means he must be some-where around here," Bella said. "It means we're on the right track. The question is whether he dropped the watch by accident or dropped it on purpose."

"What difference would it make?" Tristan asked.

"If he dropped it on purpose, it means he wants us to find him. It means he's probably in trouble and he needs to be rescued."

Tristan hadn't thought of that. "If we find something else of his," he said, "we'll know he dropped it on purpose. We'll know he's in trouble."

"And we'll know he's somewhere around here," Bella said.

They walked along the path, checking the bushes for more clues. After a while, Bella saw something and ran over to it. She picked it up and took a close look.

It was another watch, and in the centre, written in neat script, were the initials TK.

"Well," Tristan said. "At least now we know. He's in trouble. We have to save him."

The Dungeon

The dungeon that Blunt led the Time Keeper to was actually a cave in the side of a large hill. Inside, the earth floor was littered with skulls and bones.

"The bones of those who came before you," Blunt hissed. "Be warned."

There was a small, unmade bed in the cave and the Time Keeper lay down on it and realized how very tired he was. He closed his eyes and slept.

When he woke up, he noticed he was chained to the bedpost. The Thief of Time was standing close by, stroking his rat.

"What, exactly, do you need to make time?" he asked.

"My time machine," the Time Keeper said.

"Well, what do you need to make *another* time machine?" the Thief asked.

"Oh, almost everything, I'm afraid," the Time Keeper answered. It was true. So many things had gone into that machine. It had been very hard to build and he had made it so very, very long ago. "I don't even remember all the things I used," he told the Thief, "and how they were all put together."

"I see," said the Thief. "Then we'll have to use the old one, won't we? And where is this fabulous machine? Hmm?"

The Time Keeper looked at the Thief of Time. If he told him, what would he do? He'd steal the whole machine. Maybe he'd even figure out how to use it. Then he'd turn time into something you had to buy. If you wanted a short trip to the dentist, or a long vacation in the sun, you'd buy the time from the Thief. This would not be good. Those who didn't have enough money would be left with long hours at the dentist and a short, blink-of-an-eye week at the beach. This would not do at all.

"I'll ask you again," the Thief said, his voice even squeakier than usual. "*Where is the machine?*"

"I'm not going to tell you," the Time Keeper said.

"We'll see about that," the Thief said. "You'll stay in this dungeon until you tell me. You'll stay here *forever.*"

"How long is forever?" the Time Keeper asked pleasantly.

"*Forever?* It's until the end of time."

"Isn't it the end of time right now?"

"Then it's something else!" the Thief said. "I mean, *what is it,* anyway? *What is time?*"

"You can't see it, but it's always there," the Time Keeper said. "You can't change it, but it changes you."

The Thief stared blankly. "Let's go, Fluffy."

He tottered out of the cave, clutching his rat, leaving the Time Keeper alone.

The Dungeon, Again

Tristan and Bella found thirty-seven watches — a trail that led them, eventually, to a cave.

"Maybe that's where he is," Bella said.

Tristan stared at the cave. It looked exactly like the kind of cave that a giant bear would live in. But they walked into it anyway. Inside, there was an unmade bed, a lot of skulls and bones, and a watch.

"Oh no," Bella said, looking at all the bones littered inside the cave. "We're too late. He's already been . . . eaten."

Tristan picked up one of the skulls and stared at it, wondering if this had been the Time Keeper. It didn't feel the way he thought a skull would feel. When he squeezed it, it was soft. He noticed there were letters on the bottom. "It says something here," Tristan said.

"What does it say?" Bella asked.

Tristan squinted to read the small print. "Made in China," he said. "It's plastic."

They decided to keep on looking for watches after they left the cave. After quite a few finds, Tristan saw yet another watch glittering along the path. "How many is that?" he asked Bella, who was keeping track of the watches they found.

"I think it's seventy-nine," she said.

"We must be getting close," Tristan said.

"I hope so," Bella said. "I want to go home. It feels like we've been gone forever."

Tristan felt the same way. He'd almost forgotten what home was like, what his normal life had been. Bella took his hand, something she normally didn't do without being told to by their parents, and they kept walking through the forest. It occurred to Tristan that his sister wasn't so terrible. You could almost say she was nice, though you wouldn't say it out loud.

Time Flies

The Time Keeper trudged along the path with the Thief, and Blunt, and Blunt's fellow goons, Shunt, Grunt and Runt (the smallest). The Time Keeper was in chains, so it was impossible for him to run away. Not that he was a brilliant runner. He was very old, even if he didn't look it.

As you would imagine, the Time Bandits weren't the best company. Their normally bad moods were considerably worsened by having to carry the Thief, who was not a talented walker. He sat in a chair that sat on a platform and the goons struggled with the whole contraption, barely able to move.

"Are we almost there?" Blunt grunted.

"Almost *there?*" said the Thief, patting Fluffy. "We've barely left."

The goons wobbled along under their load, grumbling.

"Who said that you should be in charge of time, anyway?" the Thief asked the Time Keeper.

"I'm not in charge of time," he said. In fact, no one was in charge of it at the moment. "I don't decide how it is used. That's up to the people themselves. Do they want to spend it in the park? Or watching a TV show they've already seen? Or staring at a wall, or standing on their heads, or eating cookies in a closet, or bouncing on their beds? That's their business." This was the main problem. It wasn't where the time *went*. It was what people did with it.

"Well, you make it, so that means you're in charge," the Thief said. "Or, at least, you *were* in charge. Now I'm in charge. I suppose I'll have to change my name. Thief of Time doesn't sound right somehow. Maybe . . . how about *Lord* of Time? That's pretty good." He leaned down and looked at the goons. "What do you think, boys — Lord of Time?" They all grunted dutifully. "Or maybe *King* of Time. That sounds better. Emperor? Exalted Ruler?"

He looked at the Time Keeper. "What do you think?"

"I think Thief is probably the best name for you."

As they walked, every so often the Time Keeper would take a watch out of his large pocket, and gently toss it behind him onto the path. If people were out there looking for him, he thought, they would find his trail.

He reached in and fished out a watch and tossed it behind him as casually as he could.

"Hey, what was that?" Blunt said.

"What was what?" the Thief squeaked.

"He just threw something onto the path," Blunt said.

"Well, go and see what it is, you fool."

Blunt, who was holding up one corner of the Thief's chair, let go and started back along the path. One side of the platform dipped alarmingly and the Thief and Fluffy slid off and landed on the ground with a thump.

"You idiots!" he screeched, rubbing his sore bottom. "Fluffy, are you all right?" he shrilled, anxiously patting his pet.

Blunt came running up with something dangling from his fist. "Look at this," he said. "A watch."

"A watch!" said the Thief. "Well, that certainly is interesting. The Time Keeper throwing a watch away. And why would you do something like that? Hmm?"

"I wanted to see time fly," the Time Keeper said,

remembering the old joke.

The Thief looked at him, his tiny raisin eyes getting even smaller. "Search him!" he yelled.

Blunt and Shunt marched over and started rustling through the Time Keeper's pockets. And there they found twenty watches, what was left of the one hundred he had started out with.

"Twenty watches," the Thief said, staring at them. "You've been dropping them, haven't you? You've left a trail. A trail for whom, though? Who do you think will come and rescue you? Who would *want* to? You're not a popular man, Mr. Time Keeper. Most people are glad you're gone."

This was, the Time Keeper recognized sadly, probably true. But there must be *someone* who wanted him back. Someone who would come after him and save him. He frankly couldn't imagine Idle undertaking something like that. He couldn't imagine Idle getting out of his hammock.

"Take all his watches," the Thief commanded. "Smash them with a rock and leave them here on the road. If there is someone following us, then this will send a message. Onward!" he commanded.

On the Trail

When Tristan and Bella got to the shattered watches, they sat down and tried to count them. The watches were pretty smashed up, but they counted twenty-one. By Tristan's calculations, they had now found one hundred watches.

"Maybe he had a hundred and there's none left," Tristan said. "This tells us two things. One, we know we're on the right track. And two, we probably aren't going to get any more clues."

"They must have figured out he was leaving a trail," Bella said. "That's why they smashed the watches. But why would they smash them?" she said. "Wouldn't it have been smarter for the bad guys to leave a false trail, a trail that led to, I don't know, the edge of a cliff or something?"

"Maybe they're not very smart," Tristan said.

"But if they *are* smart," Bella said," then this *is* the false trail and they went some other way." She looked around at any other possible paths. "Maybe we should split up," she said.

"*No*," Tristan said quickly. "That's what people in movies always do and then something bad happens. We have to stick together. Plus we only have one GPS. Even if it doesn't seem to work and the batteries are dying."

"You're probably right. There doesn't seem to be any other path, so I guess we'll just stay on this one."

They walked along for a very, very long time, and Tristan began to wonder if they were going in circles.

"Bella," Tristan said, "let's assume that the Time Keeper has been captured by the Thief. Where would he take him?"

"Well," Bella said, "like you said, the Thief wants to steal time. Except there's no time to steal at the moment. What he'd want is for the Time Keeper to make more time, so he could steal it."

"So they must be going back to the time machine."

"We'd better hurry," Bella said. "Who knows what will happen if the Thief gets his hands on that machine."

The Lord of Time

The Time Keeper and his captors walked and walked, except the Thief, of course, who sat and sat. The Time Keeper hadn't told him where the time machine was, but the Thief thought that if they just kept going, they would find it. They had trudged their way through the forest and the outskirts of the very odd town where Aunt Ruth had a little mirror on her head. They had crossed vast, grassy meadows and were now in a leafy woods. The Time Keeper realized they were looping back. And they *were* getting closer to it.

"We'll find it, you know," the Thief said to the Time Keeper. "Eventually we will find it."

"It won't do you any good," the Time Keeper said. "You don't know how to operate it."

"That's why you're going to teach me."

The Time Keeper wasn't going to teach him. He

wondered if it was even possible to teach someone like the Thief. Making time was a complicated process. It wasn't like making pancakes. You couldn't learn how to do it in an afternoon. It required experience, and judgment, and patience. And the Thief didn't have any of those qualities.

The Time Keeper thought he heard a rustling in the woods. Maybe it was someone coming to rescue him, he thought. This idea, as unlikely as it was, filled him with such happiness that he couldn't help but smile. The Thief looked down at him from his chair.

"Why on earth are you smiling, you old toad? If you're smiling because you think someone is going to rescue you," he said, "you'd better forget it. You're on your own. We're *all* on our own. That's life, pal, get used to it. You don't have a family, you never had time for friends, you work alone. Who's going to come after you?"

This was all true and it made the Time Keeper sad to think of it.

"You should have made some time for yourself, genius," the Thief said.

The Thief was right, and this saddened him even more.

They finally came out of the woods and were on the road that led to the Time Keeper's barn, which made him nervous. And the Thief, unfortunately, noticed this.

"You seem a bit nervous, Mr. Time Keeper. When people get nervous, it usually means they have something to hide." The Thief knew this because he almost always had something to hide. "My hunch is we're getting near the time machine. Now, a machine like that would have to be pretty big, I'm guessing. So it would have to be in a pretty big building."

They walked along the road and passed some nice farmhouses, some biggish barns, a few cows, and then, coming into sight, a very, very, *very* big barn. The biggest barn, in fact, that the Thief had ever seen.

"That is one big barn," the Thief said. He looked at the Time Keeper. He stared at him for a very long time. Then he turned to his goons. "Blunt, Shunt, Grunt, Runt! To the barn!" He pointed to the huge red barn and the goons wobbled toward it.

When they opened the barn door, even the Thief was in awe. The time machine was the largest, shiniest, most beautiful machine he had ever seen. When the

Time Keeper looked at it, he remembered all the time he had produced: happy minutes for children to play in, leisurely hours to spend at the beach, magical seconds staring at falling stars on a summer night.

The Thief of Time looked at the machine and smiled his furry green smile.

"Goons," he said, leaning down from his platform, "I'm going to be rich."

And then he reached over and pressed the **ON** button.

The Time Machine coughed and burped and bellowed and clanged and then it settled down into a kind of purr and it began to tick. The Thief looked at all the signs for the different kinds of time: **LARGE HOURS** (learning fractions, waiting to open presents, etc.), **SHORT SECONDS** (for wondering where the time has gone), and on and on. There were dozens of them.

Now the thing about the Thief was, while he was untrustworthy and rotten and possessed all kinds of truly awful qualities you don't even want to know about, he could be pretty smart.

At the far end of the time machine was a large slot where the time came out. After pressing the **ON** button, the Thief wobbled off his platform and walked around and waited at the slot for the time to come out. He waited and waited but nothing showed up.

"Your machine doesn't even *work*," he said.

"It works," the Time Keeper said.

"Well, where is the time? I don't see anything."

"No one can see time," the Time Keeper said. "Except me, of course."

"You mean there's something there?" the Thief said, pointing to the opening where there appeared to be nothing.

The Time Keeper nodded.

"What is it?"

"It's a minute. Go ahead, pick it up."

The Thief hesitated. He reached into the slot and scooped up the invisible minute. He stared at his cupped hands. "Am I holding it?" he asked the Time Keeper.

"You are."

"So I could put it in a box?"

"If you wanted."

The Thief sent the goons off to find boxes. When they returned, the Thief set to work making time and the goons waited at the other end of the machine, scooping out invisible minutes, hours and days, then staring at their empty, hairy hands and gently laying the time into boxes.

The Thief ordered a huge tent, which he had the goons set up in the centre of town. He put up a large sign that read, **TIME! TIME! TIME! BEST PRICES FOR ANY KIND OF TIME!** Inside the tent, he set up tables where the Time Bandits would sell all the different kinds of time.

"You are no longer merely goons," he told them. "You are *salesgoons.*"

He got them clean white shirts with their names on the pockets, and gave them all peppermints so their breath didn't smell like wet dog, and gave them haircuts so they didn't look like wild animals, and then he said to them, "Now, get out there and *sell!*"

And sell they did.

The whole town lined up it seemed. And they were prepared to pay a lot, it turned out, even though they couldn't see what they were buying. When they opened the boxes, they saw nothing, but the salesgoons assured them that the time they wanted (a long hour to finish a favourite book, a short hour to visit a crazy uncle) was there.

But it wasn't.

There was more to making time than just pressing a button, but the Time Keeper hadn't told the Thief this. So the boxes they were selling were, in fact, empty. But people bought them anyway. That was the miracle. They believed there was time in those boxes. And they believed that the time (that wasn't in the boxes) would make their lives better.

Home

"Uh-oh," Tristan said, staring at the tent with its huge sign and much huger lineup. "We're too late."

"The Thief must have figured out how to use the machine," Bella said.

"Let's go look," Tristan said.

They came closer to where the people were lined up, and then circled around to the back of the tent. Tristan looked around to see if anyone was watching, and then they crept under the edge of the tent.

Inside, there were people waving money and yelling, and three salesgoons were selling time as fast as they could.

"Tristan, look," Bella whispered, pointing to the long line. "Over there. It's Mom and Dad."

How long had it been since they'd seen them? Who knows? But it was too long. Tristan knew that. Their parents looked tired and sad, and they were in a long line of tired, sad-looking people. He thought they looked older somehow.

"Should we go over there?" he asked. "Maybe they're worried about us."

"First we have to go back to the machine," said Bella. "That's probably where the Time Keeper is being held captive. He's the only one who can fix this mess."

They made their way out of town to the Time Keeper's house and when they got close they crept very quietly up to a window and peeked in.

The Time Keeper was sitting on his couch. Across from him, in a chair, was Grunt, the vilest of the goons. The Thief had them taking turns. One would guard the Time Keeper while the other three worked the tent. The Time Keeper didn't look forward to Grunt's shift, because Grunt always forgot to eat his peppermints and he had the wet-doggiest breath of all. It smelled like fifty damp pit bulls.

Grunt had fallen asleep in the chair and drool was dribbling out of the side of his mouth and pooling on the floor. He snored so loudly, the dishes rattled.

Bella boosted Tristan up against the windowsill.

"Pssst," Tristan said, not wanting to wake Grunt. "Psssst, Mr. Time Keeper."

For a minute, the Time Keeper thought he might be dreaming.

"PSSSSSSSST," Tristan said, more loudly, and the Time Keeper turned around to see a boy in the window. Tristan put his finger to his mouth and pointed to Grunt and then to the door and the Time Keeper very quietly got up and started tiptoeing across the room, careful not to slip in the puddle of drool beside Grunt.

Once outside, he whispered, "Who are you?"

"We've come to rescue you," Tristan said. "I'm Tristan and this is Bella."

"Tristan and Bella," the Time Keeper said. "I'm so happy to meet you."

"They're selling time in the town and everything's gone crazy," Tristan said. "Or it's gone crazier, I guess."

"I don't know what they're selling," Bella said. She had seen people open their empty boxes, and she was wondering if there was, in fact, any time in them.

Tristan stared at the Time Keeper hopefully. "We need a plan."

They all stood there for a moment, thinking.

"Can you make any kind of time?" Tristan asked the Time Keeper.

"Pretty much."

"So you could make a special kind of minute, for example."

"I could."

"Then I might have a plan," Tristan said.

It wasn't a happy plan. It was, in fact, a desperate plan, but it was the only one he could think of that might work.

Tristan and Bella hid in the bushes outside the Time Keeper's barn. They watched him open the side door and slip in to his time machine. They moved around to a window and peered in to see what was happening.

Inside, the Thief of Time was trying to figure out the machine. He looked up and was surprised to see the Time Keeper standing there. "Aren't you supposed to be in the house, with Grunt?" he asked.

"Yes, but he fell asleep and I thought I'd come down

here. I wanted to make a present for him and I need the Time Machine to make it."

The Thief was immediately interested and immediately suspicious. He was interested because the Time Keeper had refused to show him any of the tricks to making time, and the Thief thought that if he could learn all those tricks, he could make even more money. But he was suspicious because why would anyone give a goon a present? Even the Thief thought they were pretty vile.

"And why would you want to give that napping, useless, drooling, halfwit goon a present?" he asked.

"For precisely that reason," the Time Keeper said. "He's probably never *gotten* a present."

"He's never gotten one from me, that's for sure," the Thief said. "What are you going to give him?"

"The happiest minute of his life," the Time Keeper said. "Do you mind if I use the machine?"

"Help yourself," the Thief said, watching carefully, and thinking that if he figured out how to make the happiest minute in someone's life he could make a fortune. Imagine how much they'd pay for that!

The Time Keeper set some dials and adjusted some gauges, and turned the tweeter up and the woofer down.

He calibrated the fluorotrope and activated the autoclave and found just the right levels of dioximerd and bafflegeek, then turned the amplifier to 11. Though he was no longer young, he moved like a dancer when he worked at the machine, gracefully bouncing in front of it, tweaking and tuning and turning. It was almost like the machine was a part of him.

When he was finally ready, he pressed the button. And out came a minute, though no one could see it other than the Time Keeper.

"That's the happiest minute of Grunt's life?" the Thief asked.

The Time Keeper said, "It will be," popping it quickly into a small box.

Just then, Grunt came bursting into the barn, breathless (though not so breathless that they couldn't smell his wet-dog breath). "He's escaped! I don't know how, I don't know where, I don't . . ." He trailed off when he saw the Time Keeper standing there.

"And you let him escape, you drooling, stinky twit," the Thief said.

"I made you something," the Time Keeper said, handing the perfect minute over to Grunt.

Suddenly the Thief of Time grabbed the box out of mid-air. "Wait a minute," he said. "Why should a *goon* have the happiest moment of his life? Do you know how many happy minutes *I've* had in my life?" He stared up, thinking. "I'll tell you. NONE! *That's* how many. In all my years, I have never known a minute of happiness."

The Thief stopped to think about this. If he'd never had a happy minute, then what would the happiest minute be like? Maybe it wouldn't be that happy. It wouldn't need to be very happy to be happier than the others. But it *would* be happier than the others at least. "Who is more deserving of happiness than me?" the Thief asked. "This goon, he gets to work for *me* so he's *always* happy. He doesn't need any more happiness. I am *so* much more deserving."

Yes, thought the Time Keeper, you are so much more deserving.

The Thief lifted the lid, getting ready to be happier than he'd ever been. As soon as he opened the box, the minute started ticking away, but the Thief didn't get happier. He got something else entirely. Inside that special minute, the Time Keeper had crammed two

hundred long years. So instead of having the happiest minute of his life, the Thief of Time was rapidly getting older and older and older and more wrinkly and weirder and greyer and grumpier until, right at the sixty second mark, he disappeared altogether in a puff of dust.

Tristan and Bella, who had been watching all this from the window, ran into the barn. Even Idle had showed up.

Grunt was standing there in disbelief.

"Now, Grunt," the Time Keeper said, "I want you to go down to the tent and tell your goon friends that they no longer have to carry the Thief of Time around. You're free."

Grunt was still staring at the place where the Thief of Time had been standing only a minute ago.

"The four of you, pack up that tent," the Time Keeper said. "If you want, you can all help me get time going again. But you have to remember to eat your peppermints."

Grunt nodded and took off, running toward town.

Tristan watched Grunt loping hairily across the hills. He thought about all the problems he'd had with time, with Burt Lump, with his classes, with his parents. How there always seemed to be either too much time or not enough of it. He looked at the Time Keeper.

"What *is* time?" he asked.

The Time Keeper looked down at Tristan. "Time is what you make it," he said. "It gives shape and purpose to our lives. If there was no time, everything would happen at once."

"But why do vacations go by so fast?"

"If vacations seemed to last forever, they wouldn't be precious."

"Why does a ten-minute bus trip beside Burt Lump feel like four *hours?* Why would you make time like that?"

"I give people the time they need, not the time they want. I try to bring meaning to their lives."

Tristan pondered this. If it meant more time with Burt Lump, he could use a little less meaning in his life.

"If everything good seemed to last forever and everything bad went by in the blink of an eye, then we wouldn't care about the bad, we wouldn't even notice the bad, and eventually, bad would triumph over good. I know it doesn't always seem fair, but believe me, Tristan, it's for the best."

Tristan wasn't sure he completely understood this. But even the old system was better than what they had now, which was no system.

Time

You might remember that moment. Perhaps you're too young. The moment when time started up again. It's hard to describe. It was kind of like a sunrise where the sunlight spreads over the land and everything feels warm. The world had seemed to be in black and white, but suddenly it was in colour. But it was much more than that, so much more. It suddenly seemed like the world was filled with possibility. What could be done with all this time! It was like everyone was suddenly starting over. And this time, they'd have the time they needed to learn the piano or build a fort or read that book.

There were still complaints, of course. You've probably heard them. You've probably made them yourself. But without time, where would we be?

When they got back home, Tristan noticed that things seemed different. His parents, for instance. They were sitting in the living room, relaxing, and it was a Saturday. And it *felt* like a Saturday.

"There you two are," their mother said. "Were you gone a long time? It certainly seemed like forever. And where on earth *were* you both?"

Tristan and Bella looked at one another. Where would they start?

"Look, I have an idea," their father said. "Let's all go to the zoo."

"*Really?*" Tristan said.

"It's a perfect day for it, don't you think?" said their mother.

"Perfect," Bella said.

And Tristan realized that this was a precious moment.

Their mother looked at them both. "Maybe it's my imagination," she said, "but somehow you both seem a bit, I don't know, *older*. More grown up. Where does the time go?" she asked.

Tristan thought of telling her where it went, but decided it would take too long.

On Monday, Tristan was back at school. Here he was, back in Ms Barkley's classroom, looking at the clock (which was, at least, moving), not making friends with numbers, and getting sleepy. Ms Barkley had her watch back. Everything was exactly the same as it had been before.

Well, not *everything*. One of the good things that came out of the whole time business was that Burt Lump got blamed for everything — not just the stopped clocks, but the stopping of time itself.

"I didn't do it," he said, which was exactly what Tristan expected him to say.

It was even in the paper. LOCAL KID STEALS TIME was the headline.

And Bella now walked to the bus stop with him. That was different. And maybe he would make some friends. Actual friends, not Burt Lump kind of friends. And his parents had made time to take him to the zoo. So, in a way, the important things were different, and the other things were the same.

And time? Well, it just kept marching on.

About the Author

Don Gillmor is an award-winning writer, journalist and editor. He has several children's picture books to his credit, including *The Boy Who Ate the World (And the Girl Who Saved It)*, published by Scholastic Canada. His children's books have won many prestigious honours, including a Governor General's Award and a Mr. Christie's Book Award. *The Time Time Stopped* is Don's first foray into middle-grade fiction. He lives in Toronto with his wife and their two children.